MYSTERY OF THE EGYPTIAN SCROLL

Kid Detective Zet

SCOTT PETERS

Mystery of the Egyptian Scroll (Kid Detective Zet Book One)

Copyright © 2019 Scott Peters and Susan Wyshynski

Library of Congress Control Number: 2019907752

ISBN: 978-1-951019-04-4 (Hardcover)

ISBN: 978-0-9859852-8-8 (Paperback)

ISBN: 978-1-4783057-0-5 (Paperback)

While inspired by real events, this is a work of fiction and does not claim to be historically accurate or portray factual events or relationships. References to historical events, real persons, business establishments and real places are used fictitiously and may not be factually accurate, but rather fictionalized by the author.

Book cover design by Susan Wyshynski

First printing edition August 2012

Best Day Books For Young Readers

Visit Scott's blog, egyptabout.com, for Ancient Egypt homework resources, free teacher worksheets, mummy facts and more.

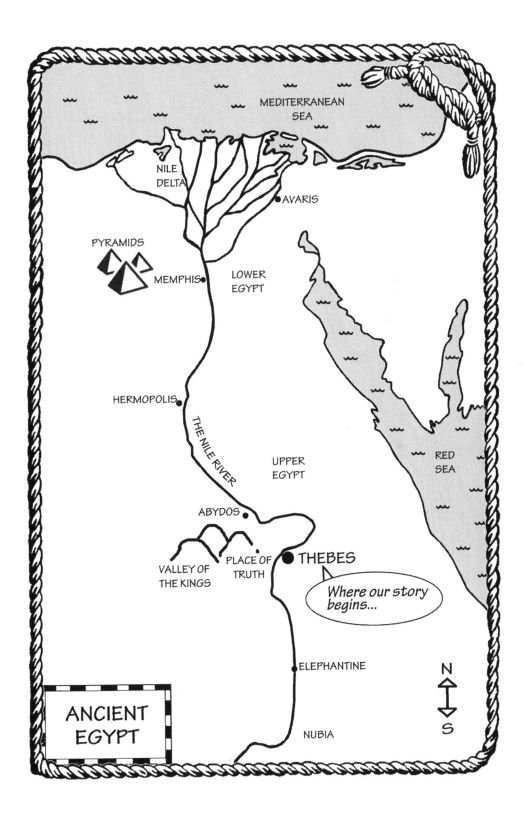

CHAPTER 1

THE THIEF

Dust hung thick over the Thebes marketplace. Standing before a mountain of clay pots, twelve-year-old Zet swatted a fly from his shoulders. The fly dive-bombed his head, and he swatted it again.

"Pots and dishes!" he shouted, waving a plate in the air.

"You're supposed to be drawing customers over here," his sister Kat said. "Not scaring them away!"

"Sorry!" Still, Zet gave one last warning swipe at the fly.

With a grin, he turned and leaped over the pots. He landed where his sister sat studying the record of trades. She didn't bother to look up. She was too busy staring at her calculations. Kat was eleven, and good with numbers and writing. Not that he'd ever tell her that.

"We need to do something," she said. "We haven't sold a single thing all day."

"Make that all week," he said.

She pushed her dark bangs from her eyes and glanced up at him. She looked worried.

"Maybe it's the heat," Zet said. "No one likes cooking when it's this hot."

"Maybe it's because we're kids?" She held up the pottery shard covered with her neatly printed hieratic. "According to these, for every week that father's been gone, sales have dropped."

She wasn't the first one to think it. Zet had been wondering the same thing. He glanced across at a vegetable seller. Under his shaded awning, two women browsed the baskets loaded with beans and cabbages. A third bartered a length of fabric for her purchases.

"If it's true, that's not fair. Our father is off fighting Hyksos to keep Egypt safe," Zet said.

Maybe Zet was a kid, but he was as capable at running a stall as any of the adults. He'd promised he could take care of his family until his father returned, and his father trusted him. Maybe they were hungrier, but they wouldn't starve. Zet wouldn't let them. So why did he have this terrible knot in his stomach?

He jumped up. "We just need to make things more interesting. I could learn to juggle. I could juggle dishes, that would bring people over."

"Yes, but there would be nothing left to buy, because everything would be broken."

"Have some faith!" Zet said.

"We should rearrange the stall."

Zet groaned. "Again?" Move the mountain of clayware a fourth time? No way. He'd already fallen for his sister's logic once too often.

"Don't make that face," Kat said. "I've been taking notes, and when certain things are placed in view, those things draw customers over and—"

A scuffle of feet and shouts broke out by the goat stall.

Zet glanced across the market square. A man, deeply tanned, head shaved and wearing a threadbare tunic, broke free of the crowd and burst into view. The man sprinted around the goat pen, glanced back, and slammed into a basket of dates. The dates flew like cockroaches in every direction.

"Stop!" the date-owner screeched.

The man kept running.

"Not this way!" Zet said, darting forward as the man bumped into a stack of pots. Zet grabbed the stack, righted it, and then flew through the air to catch a falling dish. He landed belly first, with the plate in perfect, pristine condition. He rolled over and looked for Kat.

"See that? How's that for juggling?"

Kat's eyes were on the far alley. So much for proving a point. He turned to see three medjay officers sprint into view. Two carried wooden staffs, one had a curved bronze sickle, and another had a dagger on his belt and a fiber shield in his left hand.

"Where did he go?" one officer shouted.

The date-stall owner, an old man named Salatis, pointed to where the man had disappeared. Two of the medjay tore after him. The clank of their weapons echoed down the alley and disappeared.

The third medjay stood catching his breath. He was unarmed, but his gleaming insignia marked him as important, and his fists looked big enough to crush several thieves at once. The running had winded him. Zet wondered how long they'd kept up the chase.

The medjay mopped sweat from his dark face. He bent and picked up one of the fallen baskets and handed it to Salatis.

"I'd like to ask you a few questions," the medjay said, his voice deep and rumbling.

"Why?" Salatis said.

"I wondered if you recognized the man," the medjay said.

"Me?" Salatis said, in almost a shriek.

Zet rolled his eyes. It's not like Salatis was in trouble. Still, no one wanted to be associated with thieves. That much Zet agreed with. You might get your hands cut off, or worse, your head.

"Maybe you'd sold dates to him before," the medjay said.

"How would I know?" Salatis said. "He was here and gone. And I don't remember my customers."

The medjay hooked his thumb into his kilt. "I'm not accusing you of anything, vendor. I just want some help here. Did you see his face?"

"All I saw were my dates, flying. Look at them!"

The medjay looked at the dates scattered in the dust.

"I can't barter them now, can I? Who's going to pay for this waste?"

Kat nudged her brother and whispered, "Look at Salatis, piling them into that reed basket. He's going to barter them anyway, isn't he? Even though they're all dirty!"

Zet nodded, wrinkling his nose.

The medjay's face turned red. He stepped up to Salatis and grabbed him by the collar of his dirty tunic. "Stop that. Show some respect when an officer's questioning you."

"I'm a victim here!"

"And I'm trying to do my job. I'd appreciate your cooperation. This is no ordinary thief we're hunting."

"They never are," Salatis snapped.

The medjay sighed and looked skyward. He reached into a pouch and pulled out a coin. "There's a deben of copper in it," he said, holding the shiny piece of metal to the light.

At this, Zet started. A deben of copper? The medjay was willing to pay? He shoved the plate he'd saved into Kat's arms, much to her surprise. Then he sprinted across the hot paving stones toward the officer.

CHAPTER 2
A REWARD

Standing in front of his date stall, Salatis seemed to have forgotten all about his ruined wares. He rubbed his hands together, eyes on the medjay's sparkling coin.

"Well, now, come to think of it . . ." Salatis began.

"I saw the thief!" Zet called. "I can describe him!"

The medjay wheeled, his insignia gleaming.

"Ignore that meddlesome boy!" Salatis said.

"And who might you be?" the medjay asked.

"I run the clay pot stall over there," Zet said, drawing himself up.

"And you say you saw the thief?"

Zet nodded.

The deep grooves in the man's face relaxed a little. "Go ahead. Tell me then, what did he look like?"

"The deben, first please," Zet said, holding out his hand. He knew from his father to ask a customer for money before goods were transferred.

The medjay laughed. "Pay you?"

Zet's hand dropped a little. "You told Salatis you were going to pay for it."

"Boy, if you saw something, tell me now or I'll drag you down to the office of the head medjay."

Zet's hand fell to his side.

He *had* seen the thief, and there was one distinct detail he remembered clearly. But he didn't see why he should give it up for free, just because he was a boy instead of a man. And with his father gone, he *was* the man. He needed the money as much as Salatis. More. Salatis lived alone, and Zet had not only his sister, but also his mother and his new baby brother back home.

He glanced at the stall. Kat was staring at him, open-mouthed.

He thought fast.

"All right. I'll tell you what I know, as a free gift," Zet said.

"It's not a gift, it's your duty."

Zet ignored this. "But what's the reward if I hand over the robber, too?"

The medjay laughed.

"I mean it! I want to know. If it's a good business venture, I'll undertake it."

Throwing his head back, the medjay laughed even harder. "A good business venture? Boy, I think your father taught you well in the ways of bartering. I'd offer a reward. But there's no point. You don't stand a chance of finding him."

Zet liked the way the huge medjay's eyes crinkled around the corners. Here was a fighter with a sense of humor. Even if he was laughing at Zet, he was still listening to him. Zet wondered if he'd ever be that big one day.

"Then take a gamble and give me a figure," Zet said.

"Twenty deben of copper." The medjay tossed out the huge number with a reckless grin.

Zet gasped, and so did Salatis. He could barter that for ten sacks of grain; enough to feed them for months!

The thief must have stolen something incredibly valuable! "Twenty deben!" Zet said.

"Yes. But camels have a better chance of flying than you do of seeing those twenty deben."

"Shake on it," Zet said, making sure to seal the deal.

The man's strong, leathery hand grasped Zet's and shook it.

"And where will I find you?" Zet said.

The medjay rolled his eyes. "You're a persistent one, aren't you? You'll find me at the central office. Ask for Merimose, that's my name."

"Merimose," Zet said, committing it to memory.

"Now that business is complete," Merimose said, "How about my free information?"

Zet cleared his throat. "The man you were chasing wore two different sandals."

"Two different sandals?"

Zet nodded. "They didn't match."

"That's your information? And you wanted me to pay for it?" Merimose put his thick fists on his hips. "I should cuff you for wasting my time."

But it was good information! And even if it wasn't the only information he had, it was free. Zet darted back to his stall in case Merimose tried to get in a smack or two.

"What was all that about?" Kat said, still clutching the plate.

She followed him to the back of the stall.

"Listen to this!" Zet said.

When he explained the way he'd argued with the man, Kat said he was showing off. Still, he was pretty sure she looked impressed. And that was before he told her about the reward.

"Twenty deben!" she practically shouted. "That's more than we make in three months!"

Zet grinned.

Kat looked skeptical. "But I don't see how you can find the thief."

"Think about the sandals," Zet said. "I told him they didn't match, but I didn't tell him I knew where the sandal-owner lived."

"But you don't know—" She paused. He watched the realization dawn in her eyes. "That doorstep we pass, on our way home!"

Zet nodded. "How many times have you grabbed my arm and made me look at those stupid sandals, lined up side-by-side, even though they're two different designs?"

Her mouth hung open. "Zet, that's true!" Kat's face was bright. He could see her imagining writing the entry—twenty copper deben reward for finding a thief—on her pottery shards.

"I'm going to go there," he said. "Watch the stall."

Kat grabbed her brother's wrist. "Wait."

"What is it?"

"Be careful."

"Of course I'll be careful," he scoffed. Then, seeing she was truly concerned, he grinned at her and gave her braids a tug. "Don't worry about me, little sister."

CHAPTER 3

THE STRANGER'S DOOR

Zet bounded over the pots and headed out of the marketplace.

A cool alley quickly swallowed him in shadow.

The air felt good on his hot skin. Doves cooed, nestled in eaves over doorways. Underfoot, a few sleepy pigeons rose, flapping, disturbed by the slap of his bare feet. He passed the woodcarver's open door; the sweet smell of cedar shavings floated in the stillness.

Zet flew around a corner, and then slowed. He was almost there.

What if the thief kept running right out of town, instead of going home? But then he saw the sandals, lined up on the stoop. His heart leapt. He was in luck. He could almost feel the deben in his hands. A big, heavy bag of copper. He could barter that copper for ten sacks of grain, or any manner of things. What would his mother say? She'd be so proud! And he'd tell her he was simply doing his job and taking care of them. Just like father asked.

Zet crept up the steps.

Rather than a proper door, a heavy curtain shielded the house from the alley.

He approached and gently pulled it. Just enough to peek inside.

He wanted to make completely sure it was the same person, before raising the alarm.

As he lifted the curtain, however, he suddenly realized the danger he was putting himself in. A thief lived here. No ordinary thief, according to the medjay. Zet couldn't hope for help from a passerby. The alley behind him was empty. And Zet had no weapon.

Before he could change his mind, two strong hands grabbed him by the shoulders and hauled him inside.

"What's this?" the man growled. "A spy?"

"Let go!" Zet said, struggling.

"Why should I?" he said. "What are you doing, sticking your head in my door?" His sun-darkened face was the color of old leather. A scar ran down one cheek, and mud stained his calves.

"You're a thief!" Zet said. "Let go, or you'll be in more trouble! They'll come for you!"

"Who have you led to my door?" he said.

Zet was about to say medjay, hoping the man would believe him and let him go, when a woman hurried into the room. Flour covered her hands.

"What's this? Let go of the poor boy! What's come over you?" she cried.

"He followed me," the man said, but the anger had gone out of his voice.

The woman wiped hairs from her cheek, leaving a streak of flour. She was dressed simply, and her black hair hung in a neat braid. "Why would he do that? And what's got you so upset?"

The man slumped onto a three-legged stool. "Medjay were chasing me."

"He's a thief!" Zet said.

"Will someone please tell me what's going on?" the woman said, looking from Zet to her husband and back again.

"Now, Ama," he said, "Do you really take your good husband for a thief?"

She planted a hand on his shoulder. "Of course not." She brushed away her floury prints. "What happened?"

"First, bring me and the boy some water. I think we're both thirsty from running." He looked at Zet for confirmation.

Zet nodded. Seeing the man now, he realized he was telling the truth. While he'd looked frightening in the doorway, he could see he was simply a hard worker. And the laugh lines etched deeply around his eyes and mouth spoke of kindness.

The man stood and offered Zet his stool, and went in search of another. The house smelled good, like flowers. He searched for the source of the smell and was rewarded by the sight of one of their big clay bowls on a low table, filled to the brim with fragrant, flowering herbs. The bowl was etched all around with blue water birds; funny how he remembered liking it when he was little—and now here it was like a long-lost friend. They must have bought it years ago.

The man returned, and Ama came back a moment later with three clay cups balanced on a tray of woven straw. The water tasted pure and cool, and Zet drank thirstily.

The man set down his cup.

"I'll tell you both what happened. My name is Padus. I'm a papyrus farmer. I have a plot of land on the bank of the Nile, where I tend my papyrus plants. It's a small plot, but it yields enough reeds to barter with the paper makers and feed me and my Ama here."

"Why were those medjay chasing you?" Zet said.

He smiled and held up a calloused hand. "I'm coming to that. It started when I was leaving my field. I was walking through my reeds, slowly, checking for insects and rot, that sort of thing. They're very tall this time of year—much taller than me. I overheard a man talking. I was surprised, because few people just wander into my plot." He shrugged. "There's no reason to. There's nothing worth stealing, and it's not particularly interesting, unless you're a farmer."

He took a deep sip of water, then set his cup down.

"As I said, I heard voices. Given the thick vegetation, I couldn't see who was speaking. But I did hear one man say, *Now that we have the building plans, we're set. All you need to do is to make sure our buyer is at* —" Padus paused, and color suffused his cheeks.

"At what?" Zet said.

"That's the problem. I don't know." He ran a hand over his head. Frustration was clear on his face. "That's the last I heard. I was so stupid to let them see me! I didn't think. I just stepped out into the open. And they stopped talking."

Zet groaned. If Padus had held back just a little longer, they'd be able to solve the case.

"I know," Padus said, as if reading Zet's thoughts.

"What did they look like?" Zet asked.

"One was quite fat, a large man with a short, beaded wig. Wealthy. Rings on every finger. And in one hand, he had what looked like a large scroll wrapped in leather."

"A scroll—the building plans they were talking about," Ama said.

"Exactly," Padus said. "But building plans for what, I don't know."

"What about the other man?" Zet said. "You said there were two."

"Yes. The other one was tall and thin and bony, with a long neck. He looked like a boiled chicken, if you know what I mean."

Zet grinned at this description. "So what happened after they saw you?"

"I looked at them, and they looked at me, and the fat one shouted, 'Get him!' Well, I could have told them they were trespassing, but that didn't seem like a good idea because the thin one pulled out a knife. I didn't wait to find out if he planned to use it. I just started running! I ran for town, hoping I'd lose them in the alleys."

"So then why were the medjay chasing you?"

"I think the big man must be some kind of official, because a medjay recognized him, and he yelled that I was a thief and that I'd stolen something. I was lucky to make it home."

Zet nodded. It had been close. "It's good you're a fast runner."

"That won't do me much good now, though. I'm afraid to leave my house. They've seen my face. You know what happens to thieves. And if he's official, and it's state business, it's death for certain. But if I don't leave home, how can I tend my fields?"

Ama looked stricken. "But you're innocent!"

Zet jumped to his feet. "That reminds me, you'd better bring your sandals inside!"

"Why?" Padus jumped up, hearing the warning in Zet's voice.

CHAPTER 4
THE LIST

Z et was closer to the door. He ran for it.

"I told a medjay the man they were chasing had mismatched sandals," he told Padus.

Throwing the curtain aside, Zet snatched them up. Barely had he done so when a medjay turned into the alley. Zet clutched them to his chest. The medjay glanced curiously at Zet.

"Good morning," the medjay said. His muscled shoulders shone with sweat.

"Good morning," Zet replied. "Just-er-getting my sandals here!"

"Those look a little big for your feet, boy."

"Oh! Yes. Growing into them."

The medjay stopped and scanned Zet's face more closely. "Do I know you? You look familiar."

"Me?" Just his luck. That was the thing about working in the market. People sometimes recognized him. "I don't think so."

The man grunted. After a moment he said, "Have a nice day." And he kept going.

Zet let out a huge sigh of relief and slid back into the house.

"Just on time," he said, handing them to Padus. "But keep them inside until the real thieves are caught."

"I don't see how that will happen." Padus said, rubbing his neck.

"I'm going to solve this mystery, that's how," Zet said.

Padus shot him a typical adult look. One with doubt written all over it.

"I found you, didn't I?" Zet said. "I'm already ahead of the medjay."

"That's true."

Zet said his goodbyes and told them he'd return with any good news. He left, pondering all the things he'd learned. When he reached his market stall, Kat was nearly frantic.

"You've been gone forever!"

He pulled her back into the shadows. "You won't believe what I've learned."

Crouching behind the tall piles of stacked clay pots, he told Kat everything that had happened. Her look of terror when he told her about Padus yanking him through the door was definitely satisfying. She whacked him when she realized he was scaring her on purpose. When she knew everything, she sat back, looking thoughtful.

"Let's take stock of everything we know so far," she said, reaching for her brush and ink.

"Why? It's not like I'm going to forget."

She found a scrap of broken pottery and pulled out the cake of ink. "Because it might be helpful. Maybe we'll get more ideas." Kat mixed the ink with a little water, and dipped the brush. "Go ahead, tell me what to put first."

Zet told her, and she began to write.

When she finished, the list looked like this:

Who:
Man #1 has a big belly and wears gold rings.
Man #2 is tall and thin. Looks like a boiled chicken.
Where:

Padus's Papyrus plot
What:

Large leather-wrapped scroll with building plans on it

Zet's heart leapt looking at the list. "We know a lot!"

"A lot more than the medjay," Kat said. "Do you think he'll pay for this list?"

Zet considered it. "Possibly. But I told him I'd bring him the thief."

"Well, did you get any other ideas while I was writing?"

"Maybe we should write what to do next? How about, 'Look for the two men', and then, 'Figure out why building plans are important'."

Kat added them both. "That's a good question. How could building plans be so important? Is it for a new building, I wonder?"

They pondered this, both lost in their own thoughts.

Overhead, the sun god Ra was nearing the end of his daily voyage across the sky. Soon, he would reach the horizon. Sunlight slanted across the rooftops. It bounced off the copper plates in the market stall across the way. The stall-owner sang as he gathered them up and stacked them in two locked trunks for the night.

"We'd better pack up, too," Zet said.

They draped their pots up with linen cloths, and tied the linen down. It wasn't the most secure way of closing shop, but they couldn't exactly carry everything home. And it's what their family had always done. So far, they'd been lucky. People respected the market at night, and medjay had a habit of crossing the square frequently, knowing it was full of goods.

The date-seller left just as they did.

"Goodnight, Salatis," Zet called.

"Meddlesome boy," Salatis complained.

"Uh oh," Zet said to Kat. "I guess he's not too happy with me."

"He'll get over it, the old grump," Kat said.

He hoped Kat was right. He didn't like the idea of having an enemy, especially one in his market.

On their way home, Zet and Kat kept an eye out for the two men Padus had described. They passed dozens of people. A scribe with a sack of writing tools. A barber with a box of razors and shaving oils. A woman carrying a baby in one arm and leading a goat with the other.

But none of them matched the description Padus had given.

CHAPTER 5
HOME

S oon Zet could see their doorway up ahead.

Cozy lamplight spilled through the front window into the narrow street. The air smelled of rich stew and baking bread. Zet's stomach roared with hunger. He turned to his sister and said,

"Let's not tell Mother about this, all right?"

She frowned. "Why not? You mean lie?"

"I don't mean lie. I mean, just don't mention it."

"I'm not going to keep things from her. Why should I? First, she'd probably think it was interesting. And second—"

"And second, she'd think it was dangerous, that's what she'd think! And she'd tell me not to do it!"

"Well then maybe you shouldn't. Maybe you should be focusing on the stall instead of wasting time chasing after a thief. That's the medjay's job!"

Zet stared at her open mouthed. "You were excited about it before!"

"Yes, well that was before I had to keep it all secret."

"Kat, Mother has barely been out of bed since she gave birth.

She's finally up and well enough to get around a little. I don't want to worry her! But this deben could mean a lot. Think of it! We need it."

She stared at him with that stubborn set of jaw he hated. "I am thinking of it. You'll be off running around on some wild chase, and I'll be at the stall alone. And it's hard enough getting customers with two of us!"

"I'll do both. I promise, I'll figure out a way."

Kat's lip jutted out a little, and she wound her braid around her fist. He could tell she was beginning to waver.

"Just one day," he said quickly. "Tomorrow. And if I can't figure out any more clues, we'll forget it. Deal?"

Kat blew out a breath. She glanced at their home, and back at Zet again. "Fine."

He grinned, elated.

"But just until tomorrow!" she said, rolling her eyes at his victory dance.

Over dinner, the mystery was temporarily forgotten. The family sat comfortably on overstuffed cushions before a low table. Lamplight danced on the whitewashed walls. Zet, Kat and his mother talked and laughed. It felt so good to see their mother back to her old self again.

Their baby brother, Apu, earned the most attention; he was trying to walk. The three cheered him on. The baby rewarded them by taking his first three unsteady steps. Then he squealed with delight and fell over.

Everyone wanted their turn to give him a hug of congratulations.

Later, while everyone got ready for bed, Zet knelt before the household shrine. Their statue of Bastet, the cat goddess, was small but made of the finest ebony. She had been the household god of his father, and his father's father before that. The statue had been handed down from father to son for many generations. One day it would be his. Age had softened her features. He lit a stick of incense and prayed to her for help in finding the thieves.

"Because it's not right to steal, and Padus shouldn't have to live in fear for something he did not do."

He rubbed Bastet's carved, ebony head. Even though she was a statue, he felt sure she enjoyed it.

He climbed up to the rooftop. During the very hot months, he and his sister liked to bring their sleeping pallets up there where it was cooler. Zet lay down under the vault of stars. For a long time, he tossed and turned. Finally, he pushed the linen sheet from his shoulder and sat up.

"Are you still awake?" he whispered to Kat.

"Yes," she mumbled.

"I want to go to the papyrus field. There might be a clue we're missing that the men left behind."

"Good idea. As long as you get up early and go before work."

"No. I'm going right now. What if those men go back to check and make sure they didn't leave anything?"

Kat struggled upright. He could see her staring, wide-eyed, in the moonlight. "That's exactly why you shouldn't go tonight. It's too dangerous!"

"I'll be careful," he said. He pulled on his kilt.

"I'm coming with you," Kat said.

"Forget it. Like you said, it's too dangerous."

She fastened her hair behind her neck in a low ponytail. "That's exactly why I'm coming. Someone has to keep an eye out while you search."

He had to admit it was a good idea. He could use a look-out.

He nodded. "All right. But we have to be quiet leaving."

"I know that!" she said. "I might be your younger sister, but I'm not a baby."

They crept downstairs. Zet found the oil lamp in the kitchen, along with a flint and an extra wick. Barefoot, they padded outside.

In the narrow streets, they kept to the shadows. Even though they weren't doing anything wrong, people would question why two kids were out at this hour. They didn't need strangers slowing them down with questions. They needed to move fast, before their mother awoke and found them gone.

"How far is this place?" Kat whispered.

"Past the old palace, and then down the long road that leads south out of town."

"All the way out there?"

"You're the one who said you wanted to come. Now come on, let's hurry up."

It was hard to find their way in the dark. Things looked different at night.

"I recognize that chapel," Kat said. "It's the chapel of Mut. Look, there's the goddess's Hearing Ear shrine. I'm pretty sure we turn left."

She was right. There was the niche on the chapel's side wall. Inside was the shrine with the stele—the stone carving—covered with dozens of engraved ears. During the day, the Hearing Ear shrine would often be crowded with worshipers coming to speak to the goddess. They'd ask her for favors or help with whatever ailed them. Now, it was empty.

Moments later, they were passing the old palace.

Soon, they reached the road out of town. The air smelled different. Night-blooming flowers perfumed the soft breeze. Mixed with the flowers came the brackish smell of the Nile River.

It felt strange and exciting and dangerous to be out walking at this late hour.

"I think we're almost there," Zet whispered. "He said there was a white road marker, followed by a stand of acacia." He pointed. "There's the road marker."

"And there's the stand of acacia!" Kat said.

And beyond that, they could easily see the thick shoots of papyrus rising to meet the dark sky. Zet, excited, sprinted ahead. Kat caught up quickly.

He paused before a path that led into the dark, towering plants.

CHAPTER 6

THE SEARCH

Z et looked at Kat, whose eyes were wide.

"I'm not standing guard out here, if that's what you're thinking," she said.

"Then let's go. This has to be where the men entered."

Kat stood rooted to the spot, peering into the black, murky pathway. "Maybe we should leave."

"We're not leaving! We came all this way."

"And we can just as easily go all the way back," she said. Still, she followed him into the inky tunnel of plants.

"Ow!" Zet stopped and she banged into him.

"Why did you stop?" she whispered.

"Because that's the fourth time you stepped on my ankle!" he whispered back.

"Oh. Sorry."

They carried on. Soon, the ground turned soft and muddy under their bare feet.

"Wait!" Zet whispered suddenly.

"What is it?" came Kat's frightened reply.

"We might be stepping on evidence."

Kat whacked his shoulder in the dark. "You almost scared me to death! I thought you heard someone."

"At this hour? Don't worry, we're alone," he said. *He sure hoped it.* "Let's light the lamp. Here, hold it while I do the flint."

A moment later, light sprang up. Kat's face looked eerie, all shadows and bouncing light. She set the lamp near the ground. They both got down on all fours to search. They scoured the ground for some time in silence.

"Anything?" Kat whispered.

"It's muddier up there. Keep going. I think I see something."

Sure enough, a chaotic jostle of footprints had been etched deeply into the mud.

"This must be where they saw each other!" Zet said.

There were three distinct sets of footprints. One set, whose soles didn't match, which clearly belonged to Padus.

"And look, these deeper ones must belong to the fat man," Kat reasoned. "Since he weighs more."

There was a third set; the feet were huge, but failed to make deep impressions. They had to belong to the tall thin man.

Together, Zet and Kat combed the area for other clues. He'd hoped maybe they'd left something behind, like a ring or a piece of torn fabric. Some kind of information they could use.

"Nothing," he finally said, when he'd gone over everything three times to be sure. "You?"

"Nope." Kat sounded as disappointed as he felt.

"We better go," Zet said.

He doused the lamp and they headed for the road.

"What a waste of time!" Kat said. "And I was really starting to get hopeful."

"It wasn't a complete waste of time," Zet said. "At least we know Padus was telling the truth."

"True," Kat said. "But still. What more can we possibly learn about the thieves? All we know is their description. Thebes is a big city, and even if we did see a fat man and a skinny one, there's no crime in that. It could describe dozens of people."

Zet's heart sank, because he knew what she said was true. And he'd felt so certain he could solve the case! The medjay was right. Zet had been foolish and arrogant to think he could do a better job than the official medjay.

"I guess this whole thing was a dumb idea," he said. "Sorry I dragged you out here."

He was glad Kat didn't say 'I told you so', even if she *was* obviously thinking it.

Papyrus stalks brushed his bare shoulders. The fluffy plant tops wavered overhead. Beyond them, a sea of stars sparkled in the black sky. Tomorrow he'd be back at his market stall, praying for customers. Just like any other day. Except things would be worse now. True, they were rich in pots. But one couldn't eat clay. And he'd imagined the money so clearly!

"Who passes there?" came a voice.

Kat squeaked in fright.

Zet spun, crouching, ready to attack.

At first, he saw only a pile of rags in the ditch alongside the road. But when the rags moved, he stepped closer. It was a beggar woman. Her bony arms jutted from an old linen tunic that was at least six sizes too big. Deep wrinkles lined her face, but her skin looked soft for someone who clearly spent her life outdoors, and was the color of washed linen.

"We're just on our way home," Zet said.

"I'm sorry we don't have anything to give you," Kat said. "I wish we had!"

"Thank you. You're kind," the old woman said.

Zet suddenly had an idea. "Were you here yesterday?"

The old woman nodded. "My ears were listening."

Kat and Zet looked at each other. It was a strange answer, but clearly it meant she'd been here. He could feel his heart increase in speed. Maybe she'd seen something. Maybe they'd get some more information.

"I wondered if I could ask you something?"

She nodded, and turned to him.

Silver moonlight lit her face, and he saw her fully for the first time. Although she was old and wrinkled, he could see that she must have been pretty once. But it was her strange eyes that drew his attention.

Without thinking, he sucked in his breath.

"Yes," she said. "I am blind."

"I'm sorry," he said, understanding the curious answer she'd given earlier. "We shouldn't bother you."

"Ask me your question, young man. You may be surprised by the answer."

"All right." He glanced at Kat, and then went on. "Some men came here yesterday and chased a friend of ours. Did you . . . *hear* anything?"

She smiled. "I did. My ears remember it well. The men were quite rude, as a matter of fact. One of them, a heavy fellow, cursed me." She rubbed her throat as if in remembrance. "He's not a good man."

Zet wasn't surprised to see Kat scowl at the news. She always wanted to take care of the helpless. She made a habit of putting out food for stray cats, and carrying handouts for the downtrodden.

"That's terrible!" Kat said.

Zet agreed. Then, realizing it was getting late, he told her they had to go. He couldn't help feeling disappointed. For coming such a long way, and risking their mother's anger, they hadn't learned much at all.

"Wait!" the blind woman said. "I haven't told you what I know."

"There's more?" he said, hopeful but wondering what more she could tell them, being blind.

"You sound surprised. I may no longer have my sight. But I've found ways to make the other senses keener. So let me tell you this.

First, one of the men you seek, the big one who stepped on me, smells of temple incense."

Zet nodded, taking this detail in. True, it was something they didn't know. But not particularly useful. He couldn't walk around smelling people and hope to find the thief.

"And second, his accomplice speaks with a stutter."

"A stutter!" Zet cried. "That's a good clue! We could use that!"

She smiled, satisfied, and nestled back into her rags.

"We'll bring you lunch tomorrow," Kat said suddenly.

"Good idea," Zet said. Even though it would be a busy day, he more than wanted to help this kind woman. He wanted to thank her for the information.

"Thanks are not necessary," she said. "It is I who thank you for finding the thieves."

"But we want to!" Kat said.

"You are a good girl." She paused, and after a long moment inclined her head. "I look forward to it."

Finding the thieves would not be easy; he knew it was a long shot. But the old woman had given him hope.

CHAPTER 7

THE THIN-MAN

A s they made their way home, Zet and Kat talked about the poor old woman camped along the roadside. How awful it would be to have no home.

They reached the dark city and wound through the silent streets. The paving stones felt almost cold at this time of night. They made a wrong turn into a short alleyway that stank of rotting fish and vegetables.

"Ugh," Kat said, covering her face. "Someone's using the dead-end as a garbage heap."

Plugging his nose, Zet backed out at a run.

Soon, they were back on familiar territory.

"Now that we know the thin one stutters," Zet said, "This should be easy!"

She didn't look quite as certain. Still, she said, "People probably would remember a stutter."

"Exactly! Tomorrow, we can ask everyone who comes to the stall. Someone will recognize their description."

"Everyone? I agree we should ask around, but I, for one, am not going to pester everyone. And neither should you!"

Zet laughed. "Okay, not everyone. But admit it. You're excited too!"

She grinned. "Maybe I am."

Think how proud his mother would be if he brought home the ransom! Her eyes would shine, and she'd tell him that his father would be happy to know what a good son he had.

Kat broke into his thoughts. "I can't help wondering about those building plans."

"What about them?"

"Just that they must be very important. I wonder what building the plans belong to?"

"I don't know, but you're right. What if they're for something official?"

She nodded. "I think they must be."

In the light of this, Zet felt even more urgent about finding the stolen scroll.

Back home their mother and the baby slept on. Zet and Kat tiptoed into the kitchen and cleaned their muddy feet as best they could. It was difficult in the dark. By some miracle, no one woke up. Together they crept up to the roof, thankful their departure had gone unnoticed. As soon as Zet's head hit the sheets, he nodded off to sleep. It had been a long day.

The next morning, Kat shook Zet awake.

"Come on! Mother's changing the baby."

He wiped the sleep from his eyes and groaned. "What's the big rush?"

"The third lunch. Remember? Unless you want to explain where we were last night?"

"Oh. Good point."

In the kitchen, they quickly set out three clay bowls. Into each they put chickpea salad, left over from the night before. On top of the salad went a thick hunk of bread. On top of the bread they put a handful of sweet, dried apricots.

"Can I help you in there?" their mother called.

"No!" Kat answered, quickly tying the bundles in linen.

"Hurry," Zet whispered, and shoved them into his sack.

Packed and ready to go, they said goodbye to their mother and headed outside.

Despite the early hour, hot sunshine cooked the paving stones. In some streets, laundry hung overhead on lines that attached clear across the sky—from building to building. The laundry cast rectangular shadows on the ground. In their bare feet, they hopped from one dark rectangle to the next, enjoying the coolness of the shaded spots.

Every time they met a person, Zet stopped to describe the men they were looking for. But no one had heard of them. They must have asked two dozen people. And the answer was always the same.

Kat wound her braid in her fist, then flung it over her shoulder. "I can't believe no one's seen them! No one!"

In silence, they untied the linen coverings from the neat stack of pottery dishes, bowls and pots. Zet took a stand up front. Despite Kat's warning, he still asked everyone who came to browse their wares.

A young woman who'd bought dishes there before stopped to chat with Kat. Zet's mouth dropped open when he overheard Kat ask about the two men. When the conversation broke up and Kat came out into the sunshine, Zet was grinning to himself.

"What's that look about?" she demanded.

"Nothing."

"I'm curious, too, all right? So there." She stuck out her tongue.

He broke out laughing.

Kat fetched the sack of food. "Come on, jackal-head. Let's go to Padus's field. It's lunch time."

They closed up the stall, tying sheets of linen over their wares. Zet picked up the sack of food. Time was short, so they ran most of the way. The clay pots thunked together in the bag, bouncing against his back. It was a good thing Kat had tied the bundles so tightly, or they'd have spilled everywhere.

Both gasping and out of breath, they reached the entrance to Padus's field.

The old woman smiled up at them.

"You've come back," she said.

"How did you know it was us?" Zet said.

At this, her cheeks dimpled. "Still so little trust in my powers of observation, I see!" She patted the ground kindly, like a grand-mother welcoming them to her house. Her hands were gnarled, but a fine gold chain circled her wrist.

"Come, sit," she said. "It's not often I have such loyal visitors. Let me enjoy my treat."

Together the three sat and ate, talking and laughing. The old woman asked them all about their stall in the market. She asked about their mother and father, and baby brother. She asked what it was like to be young and have the freedom to run around Thebes with quick legs and healthy, seeing eyes. They talked, eager to entertain her. She listened, rapt, hanging on their every word.

Finally the time came to go. Kat looked a little sad, and the old woman patted her hand.

"You've made me very happy today. Now go. And Zet?"

"Yes?" he said, bowing to her.

"Catch your thieves."

"I'll try," he said.

She nodded, satisfied. "I know you will give it your best."

After wrapping up their things, Zet and Kat hurried down the road. They needed to get back to their market stall. They couldn't afford to miss any buyers that might come looking to barter for some clay pots.

They had walked for several minutes, when a tall man burst out of a neighboring field. Dirt caked his calves. Scars marked his whip-like arms. His legs were long and thin.

Zet watched absently, wondering why the strange man was in such a hurry.

CHAPTER 8

THE CHASE

There came the sound of hooves approaching from behind. Zet tore his eyes from the odd looking man up ahead, and glanced back. Two donkeys approached, kicking up clouds of dry, red dust. Flies buzzed around the donkeys' furry gray ears, which flapped in earnest.

Seated on the bigger donkey was a squat man in a thick tunic.

"Hi!" Zet called as the man passed.

"Afternoon!" The man's red cheeks puffed into a grin. Up on the donkey, he jostled left and right. He looked surprisingly comfortable doing it—especially since his feet almost scraped the ground. His right hand held a rope, which pulled the second donkey along.

The animals trotted onward, tails flicking like fly-whisks.

Suddenly, up ahead, the thin-legged man stepped out into the donkeys' path.

"S-stop!" he cried.

Zet froze, his ears on alert.

"What do you want?" the donkey owner said.

"I n-n-need a ride. To t-town," the man said.

Zet gasped. He glanced at Kat, who stared back, wide-eyed.

"It's him!" she whispered. "He *does* look like a boiled chicken."

He put a hand on her arm. Was it possible the thief had walked right into their path? He thought of his prayers to Bastet the night before and said a silent *thank you.*

The thin-man grasped at the donkey's bridle. "I'm in a h-hurry!"

Zet's muscles tensed, ready for the chase. But the donkey owner kicked him away.

"Get back, dog!" he roared. "I don't like your filthy legs. And my donkey's not for rent." He kicked his animals into action and carried on down the road.

Zet let out a breath of relief. "Don't let him see we're following him."

"I won't," Kat scoffed.

They hung back, allowing the thin-man to get ahead some distance. On the open road, it was easy to keep him in view. His tall, thin shadow lurched along at a fast clip. Twice, he glanced back, seeming to take no notice of Zet or his sister.

The walls of the city rose in the distance, brown mud brick growing ever clearer. Voices of people and sounds and smells of industry filled the air: clanks of hammers, the pungent odor of the leather tannery, shouts of people offering their wares. Fishing boats clustered along the wharf. Ruddy fishermen hauled out their catch, while customers stood watching. The full nets hit the paving stones, the silver fish inside still struggling and leaping against their bonds.

Ahead, the thin-man turned into an alley.

Zet and Kat darted to catch up.

Three chatting women with marketing baskets on their arms blocked their view.

Zet and Kat squeezed past, desperate not to lose their quarry.

But the thin-man was gone.

"Quick!" Zet cried. He took off, running. An alley ran crosswise. He glanced down it just in time to catch sight of the thin-man.

"Down there!" he said, "He just turned left! Come on!"

Their bare feet slapped against the ground. A man in a gold-edged tunic growled at them to slow down. They kept running. Zet flew around a corner. He recognized the small town square with the fruit and vegetable market ahead.

"He must be up there somewhere," he said, breathing hard.

Kat kept pace with him, her keen eyes searching.

They flew into the open market. He glanced right, past the herb stall. Baskets with pyramids of colorful spices blocked any view of the far alleys.

"Split up. Meet on the other side!"

Zet wove left. Around the bags of grain. He banged into a man who was lifting a sack over his shoulder. Wheat flew everywhere. Zet's bag with the three empty bowls clattered across the ground. He snatched it up and kept running.

"Stop!" the man shouted, cursing.

Zet kept running. He glanced back over his shoulder to see if the man was following him. He didn't see the basket of lemons until he tripped over them. They rolled under his feet, sending him flying one way, his bag crashing the other.

"Boy! My lemons!" the stall owner cried.

"Sorry," Zet gasped, scrambling to his feet and taking off.

At the far end of the stalls, Kat was running to meet him. With a glance back, he spotted the man from the wheat stall, and the lemon seller. Both were red-faced. Both were running.

Both shouted, "STOP!"

Zet grabbed Kat and kept going.

"Did you see him?"

"No, you?"

"Nope."

They flew headlong until finally, the men gave up. Seeing the alley behind them was clear, they slowed to a walk and caught their breath.

"We had him!" Zet cried. "I can't believe we had him! That was our one chance. We'll never find him now."

"Zet?" Kat asked.

He glanced at his sister. Color flushed her cheeks, and her damp bangs stuck to her forehead.

"I don't know if you noticed," she said. "But that thief was really big. And really scary. What, exactly, were you going to do if we caught him?"

Zet shrugged. "I don't know. Something."

She put both hands to her glistening forehead and slowly wiped away the sweat. Then she flopped back against a wall and crossed her arms over her chest. "This is way too dangerous."

"If we'd followed him, we'd at least know where he was going. Maybe he was going to his house. We could've waited until he left and searched it for the stolen papyrus."

She bit her lip. "Maybe."

"Anyway, it doesn't matter now," Zet said, unable to hide his disappointment. "We better head back to our stall."

Glancing around, he took in the unfamiliar surroundings. They'd run far, up and down the city's maze of twisting alleys.

"Which way?" Kat said.

"We might as well go straight. Maybe we'll come to something recognizable."

CHAPTER 9
TEMPLE OF AMENEMOPET

*Z*et and Kat walked in silence, scanning for familiar landmarks.

He wondered if any customers had come to the stall. It would be just his luck that the one time they weren't there, half a dozen buyers had shown up and left empty-handed. His mother had commented last night at dinner that they were running very low on grain and beans.

Straightening his shoulders, he strode forward. Enough with this thief business. It wasn't turning out, and it might even be costing them money. He'd lost his bag with three of his mother's good bowls. She'd be crushed when she found out they were gone. Even worse, Kat was right—it was dangerous. What if Kat had been hurt? She might be a brat sometimes, but still.

He'd never forgive himself.

"Look!" Kat gasped, her fingers wrapping around his wrist and yanking him to a halt.

They'd reached a wider avenue. Crowds were coming and going. Beyond the people, great stone steps rose to the entrance of a temple. And on the steps, speaking with a young, acolyte priest, stood their thief.

"The temple of Amenemopet!" Zet said.

Despite having seen the temple once before, it was no less impressive today. Six huge statues of Pharaoh Ramses towered out front—two seated, four standing. A matching pair of stone pylons loomed on each side of a giant wooden door.

Zet's heart plummeted as the acolyte led the thief toward the entrance. They'd never be allowed in there.

Kat nodded, her face glum.

"Stay here," Zet said suddenly. He had to get in there. He had to try.

As he took off, running, Kat kept up with him. "I'm coming with you."

"No way! You're the one who said it was too dangerous!"

"I changed my mind."

Zet groaned. But there was no time to argue. They wove between pedestrians. They pounded up the steps. Six granite faces of Ramses stared down at them. The statues looked even sterner from this angle. People weren't supposed to just barge in. The temples were sacred. There were strict rules about who could enter.

So then why had the thief gone into such a holy place?

He made up his mind. He had to get inside. They reached the door. He couldn't believe their luck! The acolyte had left it ajar.

One hand on the thick wood, Zet paused and turned to his sister. "Promise me. If anything happens, run. Even if I'm caught. Agreed?"

She nodded.

He took a deep breath. He expected someone to shout at them from the street. No one did.

Pushing it open just enough to squeeze past, he and Kat slipped inside.

The hush was instant. After the noisy crowd outside, it felt as if a blanket of silence had dropped over them. Thick, sweet incense hovered in the stillness. Although the occasional chink of light shone down from holes in the roof, overall it was heavy with shadows.

Zet let his eyes adjust.

A forest of colossal pillars stood before them. Even from where he stood he counted dozens. They were spaced closely, at even intervals across the hall. Hieroglyphs had been chiseled up and down their length. Zet was unable to read the complex hieroglyphic symbols. Still, he guessed what was on those pillars.

Powerful magic. Curses to ward off intruders.

He shivered.

In the distance, he heard low voices.

Zet motioned Kat forward. Their bare feet whispered against the cool floor. They went on tiptoe from pillar to pillar. The voices grew clearer.

"I warned you not to come here!" a deep-voiced man growled.

"I had to t-t-tell you, didn't I?" came the answer.

"So he wasn't at his field. And no one knows where he lives?"

"No. I s-s-searched. And n-no one would t-t-talk to me."

So they were still looking for Padus. That's why the thin-man had been over there. But why, what were they going to do to him? A thread of fear tugged at his belly. How would Padus ever go back to his fields with these two after him?

Zet risked a peek. The two men stood in a dusty shaft of light. The big one wore a magnificent leopard skin draped over his thick shoulders. His kilt was long and expensively pleated. The belt around his waist glimmered with gold, and items of holy power hung from various loops. And just like Padus said, rings glittered on every finger. Zet had never seen so much wealth worn on a single person. The effect was almost god-like.

"Never mind," the big man said, brushing at the fur on his leopard skin. "After tomorrow night, it'll all be over. We can clean up our mess later."

Clean up their mess later?

Zet swallowed and ducked back out of sight. He didn't like that sound of that! Apparently, neither did Kat, because she'd begun to tremble all over.

"That's what I wanted to t-t-talk to you about," the thin-man said.

"Eh? What do you mean?" growled the big man.

"It's j-just, I don't know if I l-l-like—" He stopped and gulped, audibly. "If I l-l-like s-selling the plans to Pharaoh's p—p-palace."

The last was said so low, that Zet had to crane to hear it. But when he did, his jaw dropped.

"Shut your mouth," growled the large man. "And keep it shut, or I'll have to do it permanently. Don't think I won't, either. We might go back a long way, you and I, but this is the biggest deal we've had. And I don't need you mucking it up."

"B-b-but—"

There was a long silence. Then the big man broke out in a laugh.

"Don't grow a conscience on me now, old pal," the fat man's voice had grown friendly. "We'll do our deal. Stop worrying, that's your problem!" He grunted. "We just hand it over at the Rose Bark tomorrow night, and then we can forget all about it. We'll go out and celebrate. All the food and drink you could want. All right?"

Zet risked a peek.

The thin-man stared at the floor, but nodded. The other slapped him heartily on the back.

"What are you doing here?" came a man's voice, right behind Zet.

Zet turned quickly. Kat cried out as the young man seized both of them by their elbows.

It was the young acolyte priest they'd seen outside on the steps. Apart from a single sidelock of hair, braided and tied in a tight coil, the rest of his head was shaved. His tunic was of the purest white linen. He looked down with distaste at Zet and Kat's filthy legs and feet. They were both sweaty and dirty from running in the dusty streets.

"This is a holy place! You defile it with your filth!" he cried. "What are you doing in here?"

"We just—"

"Who's there?" growled the big man.

Zet gulped and looked at Kat. Her eyes were wide with terror.

CHAPTER 10

HIGH PRIEST

The acolyte yanked Zet and Kat from their hiding place behind the pillar.

"My apologies, High Priest."

High Priest? The big man with the rings was High Priest of the Temple of Amenemopet?

How was that possible? What did this mean?

The acolyte bowed low, and forced Zet and Kat to do the same. "Two children," he said, still bent forward as if speaking to the floor. "They must have snuck past me when I was returning to the steps."

"Come here, my children," the High Priest said.

"Go," the acolyte said, and shoved them forward.

Zet didn't know whether to keep bowing, so he just kept his eyes on the ground. He remembered what their friend, the beggar woman near Padus's field said: the big one smells of temple incense. Now he understood why. The sweet smell was all around them, wafting through the shadows. It mixed with his terror, making him dizzy.

This was who they were up against? The medjay, Merimose, would never believe Zet when he told him the High Priest was a thief! Zet knew they were in much bigger trouble than he could ever imagine. Not only could he never win, he and Kat might lose their lives. And the High Priest could order it done.

He wanted to run, but that would only show their guilt. So he kept walking carefully forward, keeping his eyes cast down.

Kat took Zet's hand. Her damp fingers shook.

He had to think fast. He had to say something that would get them out of there. But what? What could he say?

The High Priest made a dismissive wave with one jeweled hand at the acolyte.

"Leave us," he said.

The acolyte kept his head down. "Yes, Your Grace."

"And count yourself lucky I'm in a lenient mood," the High Priest told him. "But do not forget your duty in this holy temple. Next time, you won't get off so easy."

"I understand, Your Grace," the acolyte said. He sounded truly upset.

The High Priest waited until the young man's footsteps died away.

"So." He turned to Zet and Kat. "Come closer and let's have a look at you, shall we?"

Trying to keep his knees from knocking, Zet came forward. He stopped a few feet away from the High Priest and the now silent thin-man. Kat still held Zet's hand. Her grip was so tight, his fingers were turning numb.

"Look at me," the High Priest said. His voice was kind enough, but his eyes were like small, black stones.

Zet guessed the High Priest was trying to figure out what they'd overheard.

"Do you know where you are?" the High Priest asked.

Zet swallowed, and then nodded. "A temple," he said, deciding to play dumb.

"Not just any temple," he said. "This is the great temple of Amenemopet." He waited to see what sort of impression this made.

"Oh," Zet said.

"And do you know who I am?"

"That man, the one with the hair-lock, called you the High Priest."

"Indeed, I am."

Zet got to his knees, and dragged his sister down with him. He pressed his face to the floor. "We are so very honored. I never imagined I might be in the presence of such a great man." He didn't need to pretend to be impressed. His voice trembled of its own accord. "We . . . well we came from the fields, you see. For help."

"Ah. Indeed?" The man's voice still sounded suspicious, but a note of curiosity crept into it. "You risked the anger of the gods, and my anger, for help?"

"Yes, Your Grace."

"You are a brave boy, then. And you are farmers?"

"Look at my legs, Your Grace, and my sister's," Zet said, still speaking to the floor. "You must know that we come straight from the fields. We did not realize our filth would be a stain on this clean holiness in here."

Zet could feel the High Priest's eyes, drilling into his skull. Several moments passed. Sweat dribbled down his neck. He didn't dare move.

The man broke the silence, and there was the hint of a smile in his voice. "It's true, you are dirty. But farmers keep our good people fed. We cannot forget that. Egypt is forever grateful to our field workers. And I like bravery. It amuses me."

Zet didn't dare raise his head; he feared his relief would give them away.

The High Priest laughed. "Come now, you may rise. I'm not Pharaoh." It was clear to Zet, however, that he was enjoying his power over them. And that realization just might let them escape.

"We are too lowly to stand in your presence, Your Grace."

"Now, now," he laughed. "It was wrong of you to come here, but I will hear your petition."

Zet swallowed. "The reason we have come is because we have fallen on hard times. Our father has gone to fight in the war. My sister here and I must tend to our . . . work, by ourselves. And this has not been a good year. I don't want to burden you with our problems. They are too complicated to explain. I just want to tell you that soon, we will be in dire straits."

"The temple is not a bank," the High Priest said, annoyance creeping into his voice.

"We did not come asking for that kind of help."

"Then what is it you want?"

"We simply want your blessing. A blessing from a man as powerful as yourself. You have the ear of the gods. You have the ear of Amenemopet himself. We simply ask that you include us once in your prayers, that we may find relief from our troubles."

The High Priest stepped forward. "You are a good boy." He touched Zet's shoulder, and Kat's in turn. "I grant you my blessing. And I will do as you ask. I will put in a good word to Amenemopet for you."

"Thank you! Oh, thank you," he cried.

Kat, still clinging to Zet's hand, nodded frantically.

"Now run along. And heed what I told my acolyte. You were lucky to find me in good spirits."

"Yes, thank you again, Your Grace, thank you!" He and Kat ran for the exit.

"Boy!" the High Priest called.

Zet turned.

The fat man's face was a mask once again. His eyes looked dark and frightening, shadowed as they were in the dark hall. "Do not dare set foot in my temple again."

CHAPTER 11
AN UNWANTED VISITOR

Zet and Kat squeezed out through the temple's tall wooden door. On the steps, the acolyte priest scowled at them. But Zet was too relieved to feel very sorry for him. Still, he and Kat apologized. Then they hurried off down into the crowded boulevard.

"I was sure we were dead!" Kat gasped.

"Me too," Zet said.

"I don't know how you thought up that whole business about the field," she said.

"It was true, we were at a field, and we do need help," he said.

She started to giggle. "Oh my gosh, and he gave us his blessing and everything!"

They were running, and Zet started laughing too. One of those crazy, relieved laughs. After they'd gone a little way, their laughter sputtered out. Kat put her hand to her chest. She pulled him off to the side of the road and sank down against a wall.

"Let's just catch our breath a moment. I feel sick," she said.

"I don't feel so great myself."

With the adrenaline draining from him, he felt suddenly exhausted.

It was some time later that they roused themselves and joined the crowds.

"I can't believe he's the High Priest!" Zet whispered.

"I know," Kat said, shock clear in her voice. "He has everything. Why risk this?"

It felt like his whole world had been turned upside down. The temples had always seemed so sacred. So overwhelming. So steadfast and true. To think that the High Priest of the Temple of Amenemopet was corrupt made him feel unsteady. He didn't want to believe it. But he had no choice.

"Not all the priests are like that. Do you think?" Kat said.

Zet took a few moments to consider this. "No," he said. "No, I don't. That acolyte wasn't."

She nodded. "No, I think you're right."

"But this is bad, Kat. The High Priest, selling plans to Pharaoh's palace? I don't know what the buyer wants with them, but it can't be good."

"We have to go to the medjay," she said. "This is too big for us."

"And say what? No one would believe us."

They turned down a familiar street. They were nearing their little market, and the safe familiarity of their stall. He ran his hands along the wall of the building next to him as he walked. Then he smacked his fist into the bricks in frustration.

"You're right. For once, I agree with you. But don't get all gloating on me," he said. "I'm not going up against the High Priest of Amenemopet. But I'm not going to tell the medjay either. They'll figure it out, it's their job!"

Kat bit her lip. "Will they, though?"

"Look, we can't win! We need to get back to the stall and start trying to make some sales. I'll die if I find out customers came and we weren't there."

Business was in full swing when they reached the square.

A man was arguing with a stall-owner over the price of beer. Salatis was filling a customer's shopping basket with dates. Their own stall looked strange, still closed and wrapped in its linen sheets. One of the sellers frowned his disapproval as Zet and Kat hurried over and began to pull the covers off.

A few moments later, the sheets were folded and put away. They stood, eager to draw customers.

"Clay pots!" Zet called. "Clay pots for sale! Sturdy pots and bowls!"

Kat added her voice to his. It was nice to hear their shouts ringing off the stones. The frightening experiences they'd had over the last two days were quickly fading. He'd been crazy to strike up that bargain! Only the thought of poor Padus and his wife kept him from being happy.

"The best clay pots in Thebes!" he called, trying to sound brighter than he felt.

"Hey, boy!" called Salatis.

Zet glanced over.

"Come here," Salatis called.

Zet looked at Kat, shrugged and then crossed the distance to the date-seller's stall.

"You missed out. Someone came to your stall earlier."

It was exactly what he'd feared. After days of no sales, someone showed up the one time he was gone. "Did you tell them we'd be back?"

Salatis nodded. "They waited for you, you know," he said in a sour, disapproving voice. "For a long time."

Zet's shoulders sank. "Thanks for telling me. Something happened to keep us away. I just hope they'll come back. We really need to sell our pots."

"They weren't here for the pots."

Zet's head shot up and he stared into Salatis's cold, droopy eyes. "What did they want? Who was it?"

Salatis rubbed his stubbly chin, as if enjoying Zet's concern. "Someone asking about that thief."

"A medjay?" Zet said, heart hammering.

"Nope. Nosy as the other one, but nope. He said he was doing some special investigating. For the High Priest of Amenemopet. And that he heard about some pot-seller boasting about seeing the thief. I told him that was you. I pointed out your stall, and like I said, he waited around a long time. Seems your information is in demand, boy." He laughed, and his rough laugh turned to a fit of coughing.

"I see," Zet said. "Well, thanks for telling me." His heart slammed in his ears as he headed back to where Kat stood.

She hopped from foot to foot, anxious to hear what Salatis had said.

He told her, quickly.

Kat blanched.

"If they come back—"

"Not if. They're coming back!" Zet said. "They could be here any minute."

"What if the thin-man comes with them? What if they take us to the High Priest for questioning? He'll recognize us, he'll connect everything! He'll know why we were in the temple." Kat was shaking all over.

"We need to cover the stall. We need to leave. Now."

In a frenzy, they threw the sheets over the mountains of clay-ware. Salatis and the others looked on in surprise. The market didn't close for some time yet. Just as they tied the last piece of linen down, Zet spotted a familiar face headed their way.

"The thin-man!" he gasped. "Duck!"

"Oh, no!" Kat cried, shaking in terror as she crouched toward the back of the stall.

"He's coming." He pushed her through a narrow gap between the stacks. "Run!" he cried, struggling out after her.

CHAPTER 12
IN HIDING

Z et and Kat darted between stalls. Their neighbor vendors stepped out of the way, their mouths open in shock.

"Hey! You!" came a shout.

Zet glanced back. The thin-man had someone with him. A huge man with a knife strapped to a belt at his waist. He wore his chest bare, and his muscles bulged. Recognition dawned on the thin-man's face.

"S-s-stop!" he cried.

Zet ran for his life.

He was already spent from the last few hours. He dug deep within himself to try and find a store of energy somewhere. Kat was flagging. She'd begun to trip. He held her by the arm, dragging her along.

"Don't stop," he gasped. "Keep going."

She nodded, breathing hard.

They'd never make it home. They needed somewhere to hide. But where?

He hauled her around a corner. Then he knew.

"Quick, this way," he said.

Footsteps pounded close behind as they turned a corner, and then another. Zet and Kat were making headway, but not by much.

"Just a little further," he said. "We have to sprint."

Together, they pulled out a blast of energy from nothing. He glanced back. They'd lost the men. Together he and Kat plunged through the curtained doorway into Padus's house.

Ama was in the middle of cleaning the floor. She glanced up in surprise.

"Zet!" she said, recognizing him at once.

He was bent forward with his hands on his knees, breathing hard. "We need to hide," he said.

"Upstairs." She hurried them to the second floor. At the top was a small, bright room, filled with tools and buckets. In the center, on a great open space on the floor, lay a giant piece of thick, wet papyrus paper. Next the paper lay several mallets. A trap door led to the roof.

"There are piles of old burlap sacks up there that Padus uses for his plants. Maybe you could wrap yourselves up in them. I'm sorry I don't have a better suggestion!"

"Where's Padus?" Zet said.

"He decided to risk going to his field. A customer was meeting him, and we can't afford to lose the business."

Zet nodded, knowing exactly how Padus felt. "I hope he doesn't get caught."

They hurried onto the roof.

Rather than hiding themselves, they inched up to the edge of the building and looked down. Below, the thin-man and his burly helper wandered into the alley. They were no longer running. Instead, they looked frustrated and tired.

"How could you lose them?" the muscled man said.

"It w-w-wasn't my f-fault!"

"Let's just head back. The kids are long gone by now."

Zet breathed a sigh of relief, and Kat did the same. They rolled onto their backs and stared at the bright afternoon sky.

"We're in big trouble, huh," Kat said.

"That's for sure," Zet agreed.

They'd been pulled in deeper than he ever thought possible. This whole situation was turning into the worst, scariest mess he could ever imagine. It would ruin them. They couldn't go back to their stall. They couldn't resume their old sales.

What would they tell their mother?

They lay silent for a very long time, each of them adrift in their own frightened thoughts.

The trap door creaked open.

"I heard you were here," Padus said.

Zet nodded, not knowing what to say. He realized he was in shock.

"Why don't you two come downstairs. It's safe. No one knows where we live. No one knows you're here."

Zet helped Kat to her feet. They climbed down into the workroom with its tools. It smelled clean and earthy, like dried plants. Ama was there. Zet made the introductions, explaining that Kat was his sister.

"As brave as your brother, I see," Padus said.

"Brave or not," Ama said, looking worried, "You'd better wait here until after dark."

Padus agreed. "After sun-down, I'll do my best to see you home safely."

"What happened out there?" Ama asked, her brows knit in a frown.

Zet ran a hand through his hair and blew out a sigh.

Ama found some cushions and smiled kindly at them. "I'm sorry, that was nosy of me. Sit down and relax. You must be exhausted. I'll bring up some water, and I've just baked fresh seed cakes."

"Thank you," Zet said. He needed some time to gather his thoughts. The fact that he could no longer go back to his stall had hit him hard. Kat looked even worse. She was white as a bird's feather. He wondered if she might faint.

Ama headed down to the kitchen.

"Look at this, Kat," Zet said, pulling his sister over to Padus's work area. Zet glanced at Padus's face. "What are you working on in here? Is that paper you're making?"

Padus caught on and quickly nodded. "I like to do a little paper making of my own up here, to earn extra. In addition to growing the plants of course. I'd make more of it, but we don't have the space."

"I've always wondered how it was made," Zet said, "Haven't you, Kat?"

She swallowed, then nodded, stepping closer to the giant sheet on the floor.

"Do you want me to show you how it's done?" Padus asked.

"That would be great!" Zet said.

Padus led them to the corner where several tall stalks of papyrus rested against the wall. He explained that he first peeled away the outer fibers, to get to the soft pith inside. Using a blade, he peeled one a little to show them.

The pith inside was pale yellowish-white, and much softer.

"Then I cut the pith-core in long strips. I make them as thin as possible. Of course, the center strips are the best because they're the widest. But I try to use as much as possible."

The next step, after the strips had been cut, was to soak them in water.

"That's what's in the buckets?" Kat asked. Her color had begun to return.

He nodded. Just then Ama appeared with the snacks.

"Don't bore them with that, husband," she said.

He grinned. "They asked."

"He's not boring us," Kat said, accepting a cup of water.

Zet took a seed cake, suddenly starving. "These are delicious!" They really were. And not just because he was starving. Ama was an excellent baker.

Ama smiled.

"It's the honey," she confided. "A trader from upriver brings it to barter for the reeds."

After they'd all eaten a little, Padus carried on with his demonstration.

"Now, I lift the slices out like so, and lay them across the floor. As you can see, they're very soft and spongy."

"And almost transparent," Kat said.

"Exactly. That's what we want. Sometimes I cut them to the length I want at this point, but usually I just pound them flat like so." He hammered them with the mallet. The slices grew flatter and wider.

"The last step is simply to lay a number of them side by side in a giant sheet, overlapping just a bit. Then I add a second layer at right angles to the first. When that's done, I pound the whole sheet, and leave it to dry for around six days or so. The sugar inside the plant makes it stick together. This big piece is around half dry. When it's ready, I'll cut it up into a dozen or more sheets."

"That's a lot of work!" Kat said. "No wonder papyrus is so expensive."

Padus nodded.

"Speaking of papyrus," Zet said. "We found out what's on the stolen scroll."

CHAPTER 13
ROYAL BUILDING PLANS

Z et's words rang in the stillness of the workroom. As if unable to believe that Zet had somehow seen the stolen papyrus, Padus and Ama stared at him with their mouths wide.

Padus finally swallowed. "But how did you manage that?"

"Is that why you were being chased?"

"Yes," Zet said.

He rubbed his neck for a minute, wondering where to begin. Finally, he started at where they'd seen the thin-man on the road. He described the chase through the streets. Kat, back to her old self again, chimed in, filling in bits. When Zet described sneaking through the door into the sacred Temple of Amenemopet, Ama and Padus gasped.

"What choice did we have? We had to follow him."

"You wouldn't have gotten me to sneak in there. No way," Ama said. Her cheeks were flushed, her eyes wide with excitement. "I would've been terrified beyond belief. So what did it look like in there? The Temple of Amenemopet! Think of it," she said, turning to her husband.

He made an impressed sort of grunt and nodded for Zet to go on.

"It was all shadows, with enormous pillars. A forest of them in stone."

"And all carved with spells," Kat added. "And since we're still here, I suppose the gods must not have been too angry with us."

"No, I suppose not," Ama agreed.

"We snuck up and heard them talking. The thin-man and the big one. And the big man is the High Priest."

A shocked silence filled the workroom.

"The *High Priest?*" Padus said.

"It gets worse." Zet took a deep breath, thinking of what they'd learned about the stolen papyrus, and about how they'd been chased all the way to their stall. He picked at the thin strip of papyrus Padus had pounded as an example of how paper was made. "That scroll he stole is much more important than you'll ever guess."

"What is it?"

"The original building plans for Pharaoh's palace. They're going to sell them tomorrow."

Padus stood and began pacing the room. "Do you know what this means?"

Kat said, "That whoever buys them will know the layout of Pharaoh's home. They'll be able to get in there and steal things. The sacred relics."

"I'm afraid it might be worse than that," Padus said. "It may be about theft, you are right. But if that were the case, they'd more likely spend their efforts trying to rob the tombs. That's where the true wealth lies. Buried with the Pharaohs who've come before." He picked up one of the heavy mallets, turning it over in his hands.

"Then what?" Kat said.

"I think the most likely reason someone wants it is to make an attempt on Pharaoh's life."

Kat sucked in her breath.

"You think someone wants to kill Pharaoh?" Zet said.

"Given that the High Priest is involved, I fear this is much larger than a simple robbery. There have been rumors of unrest in the Royal House. I think it's possible we've put ourselves right in the middle of a plot to overthrow the throne."

The delicious seed cakes Zet had so greedily eaten now formed a lump in his stomach.

Ama nodded. "I agree. That palace must have all sorts of secret tunnels in it. Ways for Pharaoh to get around undisturbed, short-cuts and things. No doubt tunnels that go straight into his sleeping chamber. If someone else had access to them, it would be easy to kill him and get away."

"Not only is Pharaoh in deep trouble. We are too," Zet said. "They came to our stall, looking for us."

Kat tugged on her braids. He could see beads of sweat forming on her forehead.

"Oh, no," Ama said.

"That's why we ran. And I'm sure the thin-man saw us, and he knows now that we were the ones in the temple, that we overheard them talking." Zet pushed his fingers through his short hair. It was just hitting home now, the depth of the trouble they were in.

"We should go to the medjays," Kat said in a trembling voice. "They'll know what to do, won't they? Can't we just tell them every-thing, and we'll be safe?"

Padus shook his head. He went to the roof hatch and opened it to let out some of the stifling air. But there was no breeze, and it made little difference.

"I don't think they'd believe us," Padus said. "That's the problem. We could tell them, but it would be our word over that of the High Priest. Who do you think would win?"

The question wasn't even worth answering.

"But what can we do?" Kat cried. "There must be something!"

Zet was afraid his sister was about to start sobbing. He went and put an arm around her. She wrapped her arms around her knees and leaned into him. He thought of their abandoned stall. He loved that stall. Until this afternoon, it felt like home. Until this afternoon, it was their family's means to get by in the world. To keep hunger at bay. To keep a roof over their heads.

What would they do without it? What would he tell their father? That he'd gambled his family's safety away over the hope of some copper deben?

"We'll make it," Zet said, as much to convince her as himself. "We'll figure this out."

"You said they were going to sell the scroll," Padus said. "Let's keep our heads here. Did you get any more information on that?"

Bleary-eyed, Zet looked up. "Yes. Yes, we did. They said they were meeting someone tomorrow night at a place called the Rose Bark." Zet got to his feet. "That's it," he cried, suddenly energized. "Don't you see? All we need to do is find the Rose Bark, and bring some medjay there. They'll be caught red-handed, and we're safe!"

"The Rose Bark? I've never heard of such a place," Ama said.

They looked to Padus, who shrugged. "Neither have I. But it doesn't mean we can't find it. We have until tomorrow night, right?"

Kat nodded. The color had begun to return to her cheeks.

The sunlight that once shone through the overhead slats was quickly fading. Soon they'd be safe to leave.

They discussed a plan for tomorrow. Everyone would spend the day discreetly searching for and inquiring about the Rose Bark. Ama offered more water, and asked if they'd like to stay for dinner.

Zet and Kat shook their heads. "We'd better go—"

Before they could finish speaking, Padus leaped up and grabbed Zet by the shoulders. His face had gone white. His fingers were like vice grips.

"Does anyone else at the market know where you live?"

"I—I'm not sure!"

"Think!" Padus said, and shook him. "Do they or don't they?"

"Maybe, I never thought about—" Zet stopped. A sick feeling twisted his stomach. "Mother!" he gasped and tore for the stairs.

CHAPTER 14
A MEAGER MEAL

Zet, Kat and Padus ran from the house. They tore through the streets, all caution gone. It may have only been a few minutes. To Zet, it seemed to take forever.

Lamplight flickered through the familiar, cozy open window ahead. The three of them slowed, found an alcove and pressed themselves to the wall. The front door was shut, which Zet took as a good sign. When his mother crossed in front of the window, her movements calm and composed, he sucked in a great breath of air.

"They're not here," he said.

Padus said, "Which means you're safe for tonight. With the market empty and the vendors home for the evening, the High Priest and his men will have to wait for morning to inquire about your address. What a relief."

"Thanks for coming with us," Kat said. "And for keeping us safe today."

He patted her on the back. "Don't worry, everything will be fine. Tomorrow, we'll find this Rose Bark. We'll tell the medjay, and it will all be over. I promise."

"Thank you," she said.

Padus stood watch until they reached the front door. As Zet stepped inside, he glanced out before closing it. Their friend waved good night and disappeared into the darkness.

Kat ran to her mother and threw her arms around her waist.

"Hello," their mother said with a smile. "It's late, I was getting worried. But what's all this?" she cried as Kat stifled a sob.

"I just, I missed you, that's all," Kat said, wiping her nose and smiling up at their mother.

"Well! I missed you too, sweet one." She stroked Kat's braids. "I think you've been working too much, haven't you? I know it's a burden on you children, I wish it weren't so. But I'm proud of you. And your father would be too."

Zet stared at the floor, unable to agree, but not wanting her to see his face.

"Let's have dinner, and you can tell me all about your day," she said. "I'll just check on the baby. Wash up, and then sit down at the table, I'll be there."

They washed in silence in the kitchen. Kat looked exhausted. Zet felt exhausted.

"Let's try not to worry mother," he said.

She nodded. He wondered if they'd fool their mother. At least he'd regained his appetite. That would make her happy! She liked to see them eat well. At the table, he put on a happy face, and Kat did the same.

"Aren't you going to eat?" Zet asked his mother, after he and Kat had been served.

She waved a gentle hand. Her comforting, motherly perfume smelled faintly of baking and flowers.

"I'm not hungry," she said. "You go ahead."

"Did you eat earlier?" Kat asked, putting down her piece of bread.

"Oh, I had a little here and there. I was baking," she said vaguely.

"Mother, what's going on? Please, we want to know."

She dusted the table, smoothing her fingers over it, despite the fact it was clean. "Children, I don't suppose you made any trades today?" she finally said.

"I'm sorry," Zet said quietly. "We didn't."

She nodded. "That bread you are eating, I used the last of the wheat to bake it."

When both Zet and Kat dropped their bread on the table and looked at her in astonishment, she stretched out her arms. "Come here," she said.

The two of them sidled up to her and she gathered them close. Zet leaned into her side, wishing he were four again, and that his father was home, and that he was still running around clamoring to go outside and play.

"I only tell you this because you ask, and because you are old enough to know. You are out there running the stall, so I know you realized this might be coming." She stroked Zet's back. "But we'll get by. Something will change. The gods won't forsake us."

The sound of her voice, and the steady warmth of her hand began to comfort him. Just for now, he'd allow himself to believe they were safe. Just for now, he'd let himself relax.

"Then let's share what we have," he said. "We'll make a feast of it, together."

And somehow, once they'd divided the food between the three of them, there was more than enough. They ate and talked of old times; they shared stories about their father and all the wonderful, funny things he liked to do. Their mother told them each about what Zet and Kat had been like when they were small children, and the mischief they got into—which got gales of laughter out of them.

Despite the hard times, despite their father being gone, it was one of the best evenings Zet could ever remember. It had almost felt as though their father were with them.

On the roof, he lay and stared at the stars.

"I've been thinking about tomorrow," he told Kat.

She propped herself onto one elbow.

"It's not safe for Mother to stay here," he said.

"What should we tell her? How can we explain?"

"Here's my plan, and I think it's a good one. We need to convince mother that you and she should spend the day together. With the baby, out of the house. It's been too long since you've had time together. We'll tell her that I'll man the stall. She knows we're not busy. And then while you're out with her, you can ask around about the Rose Bark."

"Do you think she'll say yes?"

"She has to. She can't stay here, Kat!"

"I know."

"Plus, if you and I split up, we'll have more chances of finding someone who's heard of the Rose Bark, and we'll be less recognizable apart. They'll be looking for two of us."

"I'll do it. And I think it is a good idea," she said. She rolled onto her side. "Now I need to sleep. After everything, I'm just so tired."

He bid her goodnight and rolled over himself. Despite his exhaustion, he doubted he'd be able to sleep. But he drifted off shortly after, and awoke with a start as the first rays of Ra shot over the horizon.

Bleary eyed, he stumbled downstairs to find Kat in the kitchen talking with their mother.

"I think it's a wonderful idea," their mother said, beaming. "A whole day with my daughter? As long as Zet doesn't mind."

"I don't!" Zet said, grinning.

From a pile of cushions of the floor, Apu gurgled and laughed and clapped his hands.

Kat went over and swept him up. "And you agree!" she cried, swinging him in a circle.

Since this was currently Apu's favorite thing, to be swung around and around, he shrieked in delight. Zet took a turn too. When he finally handed his baby brother over to their mom so she could get the child ready for his outing, Kat pulled him aside.

"You're not going back to the stall today, are you?" she whispered.

CHAPTER 15
WHAT REMAINED

Z et and Kat faced off in the kitchen. She looked furious that he'd even think of going back to the stall.

"The thin-man knows it was us! He'll come back! You can't possibly be stupid enough to go back." She was so upset, her face was red.

He shrugged. "I might. Just for a little while."

"It's too dangerous! We were lucky to get away!"

"And we need to eat. What do you want me to do, Kat? Let us starve? I promised father I'd take care of us. So don't call me stupid. I'll do what I have to." He knew he sounded sullen, and he didn't care. It was the truth.

Kat was beyond angry. She looked terrified. "Where will we meet?" she said, changing the subject.

He thought about it for a moment. "The Chapel of Mut. Meet me near the shrine of the hearing ears. Do you remember where it is? You pointed it out that night, when we were going to the papyrus field."

"Of course. What time?" she said quickly. Their mother was coming.

"Sun down."

"And if you're not there?" she said, her brows tented in fear. "What then?"

"I'll be there."

"What's all this whispering?" their mother said with a good-natured laugh. "It sounds as if you were plotting some big secret!"

Zet managed a grin, although inside he felt like his world was falling apart. "I better get going! Have to get to the stall on time."

"Thank you, Zet," she said, handing him a package. "Lunch. Dried fruit mostly," she said.

Looking into her eyes, he knew then that despite her smile and light-hearted tone, she felt as worried as he did. And out of everything, that frightened him the most.

"Have a good day!" she called.

"You too!" he called back, and ran from the front door. He couldn't bear to see her that way.

Please, let me sell at least one pot. Please. Just one.

He prayed like that as he walked. At the woodcarver's house, he paused before the open door. The man crouched and chiseled at the lid of a half-completed, ornate trunk. Sweet-smelling cedar-wood dust hung in the hot air.

"Excuse me?" Zet said.

The shirtless man glanced up. He wiped a bead of sweat from his brow.

"I'm looking for a place called the Rose Bark. Do you know where it is?"

The woodcarver thought for a moment. He shook his head. "Nope, sorry."

Zet carried on. He asked dozens of people as he went. No one had heard of the place. It was strange. Thebes was big, but someone had to have heard of it.

He took the long way around, cutting north up two extra streets. He approached the market from a different angle to get a clear view of his stall. He wanted to check things out in advance, from a distance. Who knew if men would be posted up, waiting for him?

To his relief, all was calm.

It was just like any other day. Blue sky crowned the hot square. The dusty, shuffling sounds of morning preparations were like a balm to his soul. Soothed by the familiarity, he padded across the paving stones to his family's beloved business.

The other vendors greeted him, curious but friendly enough.

It was only as he drew closer that he noticed something was wrong. The linen sheets that covered their precious wares hung at odd angles. The tall, covered stacks were shaped differently. Shorter. Lumpier. Bulging in odd places.

A tremor of fear started in his belly. It spread outward, claiming his arms and legs, making his head spin. His hearing went all funny, as if he were going to pass out. He forced his legs forward. Faster. Sweating, he broke into a run.

With both hands, he yanked the closest sheet up.

Broken pottery shards spilled out. An avalanche of them. Tumbling and clattering and smashing to the ground. Zet stumbled backward, pulling the sheet with him. Nothing was recognizable as having once been a beautiful dish or pot. Instead, he faced a mountain of destruction. He fell to his knees, clutching the sheet to his face. He nearly threw up.

Zet forced himself to his feet. He ran to the other covered piles. Pulled the sheets free. By now, every vendor had abandoned their stall to come and stare in horror.

"Who could have done such a thing?" the goat-vendor cried.

So much beautiful work had gone into making the earthenware. Zet and his father had often made trips downriver to purchase the items in bulk from the artisans who made them. To see it destroyed was sickening.

Forcing back tears, he crunched over the remains. One item caught his eye: a shard with Kat's handwriting on it. He bent and picked it up.

Their list.

They thought they'd been so clever, making a list with all the facts of the case. He dropped it and crushed it underfoot.

"Fetch the medjay, boy!" said a spice-merchant. "This is an outrage to all of us!"

Zet glanced up at him, barely registering the gathering crowd. With a nod, he left the square. But he had no intention of fetching the medjay. For all he knew, they were on the High Priest's side now and they'd take him into custody. If that happened, he'd have no hope of stopping the meeting at the Rose Bark.

Shaken, he forced the horror of what he'd seen from his mind. Because if he thought about it, he'd break down and wouldn't be able to carry on.

He was angry. He was frightened. And he was determined to put an end to this.

The morning passed in a blur. Zet went everywhere. He felt as if he asked every person in Thebes about the Rose Bark. No one knew if it was a tavern or a shop or a little square with a tree in it. No one had ever heard of it.

The whole thing was beginning to baffle him. It was too strange. How could no one have heard of the place?

It felt like a dead end.

Not knowing what else to do, he decided to head for Padus and Ama's house. He slipped through the familiar heavy curtain. With relief, he found he was in luck. They were both home.

"We both just came in ourselves," Padus said.

Ama called them into the kitchen. "This is a stand-and-eat lunch," she said, laying out some dried meat and bread, and pouring water for the three of them.

Zet pulled out his packet of dried fruit, but Ama told him to save it for later when he might need it. They still had a well-stocked pantry, and she'd make sure he was full before he left. He nodded in gratitude.

The three of them settled in to compare stories.

CHAPTER 16

TRANSFORMATION

As it turned out, Zet, Padus and Ama had all had similar experiences trying to find the mysterious location.

"No one has heard of it!" Ama said.

"I'm beginning to think it's more complicated than it seemed," Padus said, rubbing his chin.

"What do you mean?" Zet asked.

"Maybe it's a code of some sort?" Padus said.

"If that's the case . . ." Zet trailed off. A code? They had no time to break a code. Not without some further clues as to its meaning. And how would they manage that? It was past midday. The meeting at sunset was now only hours away. They had no hope.

His mind went to his stall. Frustration took over. He put his water cup down harder than he meant to. It slammed against the wooden table.

Ama jumped.

"Zet," she said, looking at his face. "What is it? What's happened?"

He sighed and put his fingers to his eye-sockets, trying to rub away the nightmarish vision of what he'd seen. Finally, he let his hands drop, and he met their curious stares.

"It's our stall," he began.

He told them of the destruction. Their mouths dropped, and their faces turned white as sheets.

"Buying new pots would cost a fortune. We'd never be able to do it. My father trusted me. My family has been selling clayware there for generations. And in two days I lost it all. What am I going to do?"

"Something," Padus said. "We're all going to pick ourselves up and think of something!"

"Not to make things worse than they already are," Ama said, "But I overheard a medjay asking about you, Zet. Apparently they're searching for you. It's too dangerous for you to go back out!"

Zet toyed with his cup, turning it slowly. Padus started pacing. Ama cleared the lunch things away.

Needing some space to think, Zet wandered out into the front room. He pulled the curtain aside a few inches and stared into the street. The silence of post-midday-mealtime had settled on the city. Many people were napping, waiting for the world to cool down. With Ra, the sun-god, at his high point in the sky, the heat was almost unbearable. It radiated up from the sun-bleached paving stones.

Zet felt eyes watching him. Glancing up, he caught sight of a cat nestled under the shady overhang of a rooftop. They stared at one another for a time. Then the cat closed its feline eyes, but Zet knew it was still aware, still watching him with some sixth sense, in the way cats seem to do.

He turned his attention back to the deserted street. How could no one in the city know of the Rose Bark?

It was a riddle. A question with no answer. He had no time to go down that route any longer. He needed to switch paths. And he had an idea.

"Ama!" he called, hurrying into the kitchen.

She turned, wiping her hands on a cloth.

"Ama, I need you to shave my head."

Clearly this was the last request she was expecting.

"And Padus, can you write?"

"Of course! I may be a lowly farmer, but as a papyrus maker, I made it a point to learn the craft of writing."

"I have a great favor to ask of you."

"Name it. Whatever I have is at your disposal," Padus said.

"I need you to write a letter."

When he'd told them his plan, they agreed that although it was dangerous, it was the best hope they had. In addition to the shaved head, Ama had a few ideas of her own to add to Zet's trans-formation.

Letter in hand, Zet stepped out the door. To any observer, he no longer looked like the boy who manned the pottery stall in the market. He looked like an official city courier. The dark waves of hair that his mother loved were gone. Instead, his head was clean-shaven. Thick black lines of kohl surrounded his eyes. At his waist, he wore a belt of blue-dyed fabric, which Ama had made by folding one of her scarves. She attached a leather pouch at his hip, and made a number of loops for holding things at the back. One of the loops held the letter Zet had dictated to Padus.

He looked so official, Ama worried someone would stop him and ask for his services.

"Don't worry," Zet said. "I'll be running too fast for that to happen."

They wished him good luck.

"Thank you," he said, and sped out the door.

It wasn't long before he reached the office of the medjay. He slowed, his heart pounding at the sight of all those officers coming and going. Sweat trickled down his ribs.

It was now or never.

Summoning his courage, he strode the last few steps to the door. A medjay was exiting just as Zet came up the low steps. Zet started when he realized the man looked familiar. It was the muscular thug who'd come looking for him with the thin-man the day before. But today, the thug was in uniform.

Zet's mind screamed, *run!* But he stayed his ground, praying the costume worked.

It did. The thug shoved past with barely a glance and headed into the street.

Inside he found himself in a front office. He approached a desk, where an official sat making notes on shards of white ostraca. The official glanced up.

"Got a message?" he said.

"Yes. It's for Merimose, the head medjay." Sweat poured down his sides, but not from running. Zet hoped the man wouldn't notice he was sweating in fear.

"Give it to me, Merimose is out of the office."

Zet expected this to be the case, which is why he'd written it all down. Everything—about the High Priest, about the stolen plans to Pharaoh's palace. So that if he was caught today, Merimose might still have a chance of working things out. And if he did, he'd know Zet was telling the truth.

"When will he be back?" Zet said.

"The day after tomorrow."

CHAPTER 17

THE MIGHTY BULL

Z et stood before the officer, reeling at the news.

"You're certain?" Zet said. "Gone until the day after tomorrow?"

The officer looked suddenly curious. "Why, what's it to you, boy?"

"It's just, my orders are that the document is important. He needs to see it today!"

"They're all important. That's the way it is in this office."

"But this one . . ." Zet paused. "Are you sure there's no chance of him coming back today?"

"Not a hope. He's on the opposite bank, investigating a crime in the tomb builder's village." The man gestured in the general direction of the Nile.

Zet knew that if you stood on the bank and squinted into the distance, you could see brown, desert hills. Egypt's Pharaohs were buried in those hills, in secret tombs, but he knew little more about them than that. What he did know was that it took hours to get there from here. He had no chance of going to the tomb builder's village to find Merimose. Not now, it was too late.

If what the man said was true, he was completely out of luck.

"I see," Zet said.

"Give it to me, I'll put it in his box," the man said.

What else could Zet do? He handed over the sealed scroll and watched the man set it into a small cubby.

"Is there anything else?" the officer said.

Zet shifted from one foot to the other. Should he tell him? Should he trust this man? The sun was a good deal past noon. Time was running out. He swallowed.

"No," Zet said. "No, thank you. I'd better get on with my work."

The man nodded and turned back to writing on his ostraca shards.

Wandering out into the streets, Zet tried to think what to do. He'd barely gone two blocks when he cursed himself for handing over the papyrus. He should have taken it to the palace! He could have entered as a messenger, and handed it to one of Pharaoh's own men!

Maybe it wasn't too late. He could have Padus make another.

When he reached Padus's street, however, medjay swarmed the narrow lane.

"It's that house," a woman was saying. "He's the one with the two different sandals. He used to leave them on the step all the time."

Zet hung back and watched in horror as two big, armed medjay entered through Padus's curtain. He heard Ama's cries. Then, a moment later, the men came out with Padus between them. Zet's stomach almost heaved at the horror.

They would kill him. Impale him on a stake, or burn him to death. That was the punishment for crimes against the state. And it was Zet's fault. He was the one who'd given Merimose the clue that had eventually led the men to Padus's door.

Padus turned and Zet stepped fully into the alley. Their eyes met. Padus made a tiny movement with his head.

No, his friend's eyes said. *Don't give yourself away.*

A medjay remained on guard in front of Ama and Padus's house. The others marched Padus right past where Zet stood. He could have reached out and touched his friend, they were so close. But there was nothing Zet could do. A suppressed cry caught in his throat.

His whole world had fallen to pieces.

All because he'd sprinted across the square two days ago, on that cursed afternoon, in hopes of a handful of copper deben.

Zet's feet carried him to the palace. He didn't know what he was going to do; he simply hoped the answer would present itself. Men marched up and down in front of the grand entryway. He approached the first one he saw and tried to explain he had an important message for Pharaoh.

"Where's your scroll, boy? Or an ostraca?" the guard asked, his eyes searching for the expected item.

"That's just it, I'm to give the message by word of mouth."

"No one gives Pharaoh messages by word of mouth. Get away from my gate."

At that moment, trumpets sounded.

Weapons clanked as men rushed into position.

"Pharaoh's coming, make way!" said a man.

Zet darted back, pressing himself to the ground.

A procession appeared, marching down the wide boulevard. First came a handful of royal soldiers, with swords at their waists and pectorals over their chests made of hammered silver and inlaid with gold. Then came ladies, some carried on litters, others walking, all in gowns of white and trimmed with precious metals and jewels. They chatted and fanned their faces, laughing. In a large litter, carried by six powerful men, sat the Mighty Bull, the Great God on Earth.

Pharaoh himself.

The curtains had been pulled back, so all might look upon him.

It was a rare glimpse, and one Zet had never dreamed of experiencing. Not only did Pharaoh normally remain hidden from his people, with the war in Hyksos, he'd been traveling much of late. Rumor was that he'd spent a good deal of time leading the soldiers himself, but that he'd come back now to deal with matters of state.

Zet raised his head for a better look, and at that moment the Mighty Bull happened to glance down. Their eyes met.

Pharaoh's were dark and his lids were heavily painted with green malachite, gold dust, and black carbon. Despite the overwhelming glory of his appearance, it couldn't hide the bluish pouches under the Great One's eyes.

The Mighty Bull looked worn, and Zet wondered if he knew of the plot on his life. Surely he'd heard of the royal scheming, if Padus had known of it. Between that and the war, it must be taking its toll. Even on one so great.

Zet had no idea why he did it, but despite everything, he smiled at Pharaoh. To his utter surprise, Pharaoh smiled back. His eyes crinkled at the corners, causing the make-up to bunch into little wrinkles. The Great One raised a jeweled hand, as if waving and blessing Zet all at once.

The action emboldened Zet.

This was his chance. He had to warn Pharaoh!

He stood. As he did, a guard shot out as if from nowhere and grabbed him by the arm.

"Get back," he ordered.

In the next instant, the litter had passed through the gates. Pharaoh was gone. The doors clanged shut once again. His opportunity was lost.

"Get moving, or I'll cite you for causing a disturbance," said the guard, still crushing Zet's arm in his powerful grip.

Zet glanced at the fingers and the man let go.

"I know that was an amazing sight for a boy like you," he said. "Now run along. You'll have a good memory to tell your friends and family."

Out there in the street, Zet realized he had nowhere to run along to.

He'd lost his family business. They couldn't go home, they could never go home. Even once today was over, the High Priest would track him down and kill him and his family. A man like that wouldn't want witnesses. And he couldn't go to Padus and Ama's. They'd been caught, too.

He thought of his childhood friends. His best friend Hui had left home several months ago to become an apprentice at the Kemet Workshop. Hui might have had some idea what to do. As for the others, there was no way he'd even think to bring them into this nightmare.

His life as he knew it was over.

The thought nearly crushed the breath from his chest. He and his mother, sister and baby brother would have to leave town with nothing. But where would they sleep? How would they eat?

How would his father ever find them?

Zet wanted to lie down right then and there. He wanted to escape into a corner, curl up into a ball and close his eyes against the world.

Instead, he stumbled down to the Nile.

CHAPTER 18

UNDERSTANDING

The broad river sparkled up ahead. Zet headed for it.

He had a vague idea of finding a boat headed for the far bank. Maybe he'd find a person who was headed for the tomb maker's village. Maybe they could carry a message to Merimose for him. Saying what, he had no idea. And the chance of finding someone to help was next to impossible.

Time was ticking away. He'd need to meet Kat and his mother and baby brother soon. She'd be worried if he didn't show up. And he needed to prevent them from going home at all costs. But he still had a little time.

Around the curve in the river, he spotted the crowded water-steps. Near the fishing boats, skiffs made of papyrus stood ready to taxi passengers up and down river, or across to the far bank. Zet approached, drawing ever closer as the events of the last two days roiled around in his mind.

Something was bothering him. Some little thing that he couldn't quite grasp.

He tried to figure out what it was. He went over the facts, but the point he was searching for kept eluding him. A ferryman helped two passengers onto a skiff. A second boat pulled up to the steps and threw out a line. A boy caught it and tied the rope to an iron cleat, which was fastened to the stone stairs. Further down, three fishermen scrubbed the deck of their vessel.

Then he had it.

The Rose Bark.

Bark was another word for boat.

His feet carried him flying to the shore. He skidded to a halt in front of the fishing boat with the three men on board. It was a large skiff made of papyrus reeds tightly lashed together.

"Hey!" he shouted.

The nearest man glanced up. His face was deeply tanned. He quirked his brow.

"I'm looking for the Rose Bark!"

The fisherman wiped sweat from his face with his forearm. "The Rose Bark?" he said, as if searching his memory. He turned to the others. "Do you know it?"

They shook their heads.

"Sorry, messenger," he called. "We don't usually dock in Thebes. Try that boat down there. Maybe the captain knows it."

"Thanks," Zet called back.

He headed for the boat. It was larger than the others, and unlike most it was made of wood. Cedar planks, glued with resin, and it had a large square sail made of linen cloth.

"Hello?" Zet called.

He waited.

"Hello!" he shouted a second time.

"Coming, coming," said a reedy voice. A little old man poked his head over the side. He wore a wig, but it was all off kilter. He looked like he'd been sleeping. His eyes lit up at the sight of Zet. "Oh good. You have a message for me?"

"I'm sorry to say I don't."

The old man's scrawny shoulders drooped a little. He reminded Zet of a friendly, bony cat, all lean with big dark eyes. "Oh. That's a disappointment. Can I help you with something, then?"

"I'm looking for the Rose Bark."

"Rose Bark . . . Rose Bark . . ." he put a finger to his lips. "Aha!" he raised his finger in the air. "I have it! You must mean the boat with the roses painted along the hull. Am I right?"

"I'm not sure! That's all I know, that I need to get to the Rose Bark."

The old man shot Zet a toothless grin. "Then I woke up for a good reason. Always nice to help a fellow in need. Yes, it's the boat with the roses you want. Only one that would match that description. Roses painted all down each side, twining into each other if you know what I mean. Pretty thing it is."

Zet's heart was in his throat. Finally. Finally someone knew of it!

"Where can I find it?"

"Some official owns it. Try down near Pharaoh's palace. At that set of water-steps where the nobles like to dock."

"Thank you so much!" Zet cried.

The old man laughed and waved. "Glad to be of service!"

Overhead, the sun-god was sailing swiftly for the horizon. Cool shadows slanted across the waterfront. He needed to get to Kat and his mother soon. They'd be waiting outside the Chapel of Mut, as planned.

As he made his way there, Zet went over everything in his mind. He thought about his family, their stall destroyed. He thought about poor Padus, locked up in jail and awaiting death; and Ama, home alone and terrified. He thought of Pharaoh with his kind, world-weary eyes, and the threat on his life. And then he thought of the medjay, Merimose, called away to a village in the desert.

It's true, he knew of the Rose Bark now. But what he would do with that information he had yet to figure out. Everything he knew and cared about had fallen into ruin. And it seemed there was nowhere to turn for help. No one would believe a boy like him. And the man in power, the High Priest, wanted him dead.

CHAPTER 19
A DECISION

Kat, their mother and little Apu were already outside the chapel, waiting. He spotted them from a distance, seated to the right of the Hearing Shrine. Zet's heart swelled at the sight of his family. And at the same time, he wondered if this was a foretelling of things to come. Would they be left to the streets, the four of them, their happy home gone forever?

Apu saw Zet first. The baby gurgled and clapped his chubby hands. Zet swept him up and hugged Apu tight. Their mother was smiling, but her smile faded at Zet's appearance.

"Your hair," she cried, touching his shaved head. "And this uniform, what's going on?"

Zet desperately wanted to lie. He wanted to tell her everything was fine. But what excuse could he give for not letting her go home?

He let out a huge breath. "I have to tell you something. And it's not good."

Kat was shaking her head frantically, but Zet ignored her.

His mother's eyes were wide. "Did something happen with the stall?"

Apu was touching Zet's face paint with a curious finger. Zet sat down against the wall, still holding his baby brother.

"Do you remember how father asked me to take care of things while he was gone? And you were still in your birth bed, and Apu was only days old and I said I would?"

"Of course!"

"And you both trusted me? That I could do it?"

At this point, Kat had her face in her hands, as if she couldn't bear to hear what he was going to say next. A woman with a marketing basket approached the Hearing Ear shrine. She made an offering, and spoke in low tones. Zet waited for her to leave, and took another deep breath.

"Here's the thing," he said. "I need you to keep trusting me. Just for tonight. Something has happened, many things. Terrible things. All I ask is that you let me try to deal with them now, without asking questions."

His mother studied his face. "Perhaps I could help you."

"No." He shook his head. "It's something only I can fix."

"If there are terrible things, I'd like to know about them. I'm your mother."

He wished he hadn't used those words, because now it was clear she was curious and worried. He stood and handed her the baby. "I know you'll be angry with me when I tell you there isn't time, but that's the truth. I have to go. Right now. And you'll be even angrier when I tell you that you can't go home tonight, but you can't. Men are looking for me. Evil men. And they'll hurt anyone they find at our house. That's why I'm dressed in this disguise."

"This can't be true! What could you have possibly done? I don't believe it. You're exaggerating."

"Look at Kat's face. See how scared she is?"

It was true, Kat had begun to shake, knowing it had come to this. They couldn't go home. They were stuck in the street.

"Kat knows it's true. That's why she took you out today. I'm sorry we created this lie to get you out of the house, but I love you and am terrified for you, for all of us."

"Men are after you? At least give me some hint why!"

Zet glanced at the sun. It was nearly at the horizon. He drew himself up to his fullest height. The time for arguing was over. "If you love me, if you love this family, you'll do what I say. You'll let me go, and you'll stay away from our house. What is your decision, Mother?"

She looked taken aback.

"I'm running out of time!" he said.

"All right." She nodded, quickly. "Clearly, you give me no choice. I'm not happy, but we'll stay here, we'll wait for you."

"Thank you!" He threw his arms around her neck and kissed her cheek. She smelled of flowers. She smelled of home. She smelled of everything good he stood to lose.

"I'm coming with you," Kat said.

"No. It's too dangerous. I'll be back as soon as I can." Zet turned and sprinted away.

He heard footsteps and turned to see Kat running after him. He slowed to let her catch up. "Kat, I mean it! It's too dangerous."

"It's my responsibility, too," she said. "So don't argue. And you'll need help. And I'm not going to sit around when our family is in trouble."

He groaned, but kept going.

"Where are we going? Did you find out about the Rose Bark?"

He told her everything as they ran. About their pots being destroyed, and how he'd found them all smashed to pieces. He told her about meeting the Pharaoh in the street. About Padus and Ama. About the papyrus he'd tried to deliver to the medjay. And about the discovery that the Rose Bark wasn't a restaurant, or a tree, but that it was a boat.

Suddenly, he saw it.

"Out there, on the water!" Zet cried. "Look!"

Sure enough, there it was. A lavish, private river cruiser. The boat was long and crafted of cedar. Its sail was unfurled, and a gentle breeze tugged it shoreward. All along the side of the boat, below the polished rail, were beautifully painted roses. Leaves and stems twined around them, so that it looked like it was festooned with a long garland of flowers. The prow, which arched upward in a graceful curve, was crown by the head of a wooden ibis bird.

Kat caught her breath. "It's beautiful," she said.

Together they stood watching in awe. It made a beautiful picture. On the Nile's opposite bank, mountain peaks cradled the setting sun. Overhead, long streaks of red and purple stained the sky. There was very little wind. Water lapped gently at the stone wall that bordered the river, and the air smelled fresh. The sun winked, sparkling. Then it dropped out of sight.

From the pier-side, two men strode into view—the High Priest and the thin-man. The High Priest wore a gilt-edged, ankle-length kilt, which had been pressed into countless knife-sharp pleats. The thin-man followed close behind, his sandals flapping as he walked. Over one shoulder, he carried a large basket filled with what appeared to be the makings of a lavish picnic. Zet had no doubt that secreted beneath the fruits and flagon of wine was the precious scroll, well-wrapped in leather to keep it safe.

The High Priest turned, as if sensing someone watching.

"Get back," Zet said, grabbing Kat's hand and pulling her behind a pile of reed baskets.

CHAPTER 20

THE ROSE BARK

Zet and Kat ducked back just in time.

The High Priest scanned the waterfront. Behind the baskets, Zet held his breath. The air smelled of old fish. He wanted to gag. After a moment, the priest glanced away, turning his attention to the boat.

On the water, the boat came closer. A tent-like structure occupied much of the boat's deck. Colored ribbons flew from its four corners, and the sides were trimmed with thousands of golden beads. Four servants guided it shoreward, using long paddles. One leapt out when they reached the water-steps. A second threw out ropes, and the servant on shore fastened the boat in place.

When the boat came to a gentle halt, the curtains of the tent were thrust aside.

Out stepped a man with broad, muscular shoulders, on which rested a collar of shining gold. A striped cloth covered his head, held in place with a gleaming circlet. Everything about him seemed regal. There was a grace and power with which he surveyed his deck. His servants bowed low, but he brushed them aside, ordering them ashore.

The tent flap was pushed aside a second time, and a beautiful young woman stepped out. A white sheath hugged her slim upper body; it flowed away in billows down her legs. Around her shoulders lay a delicate, short cape that looked as if it had been sewn from threads of pure gold. A formal, black wig with beads of turquoise framed her high cheekbones. Her wide, almond shaped eyes looked neither cunning nor evil, and Zet wondered if she was aware of the purpose of the meeting.

Beside him, Kat sighed at the sight of her.

"Who is she?" Kat whispered.

"I don't know. Look, the man's inviting the High Priest and the thin-man on board. This is it, Kat."

"What are we supposed to do? We can't just run over there!" she said.

That was just it. He didn't know what to do. It could all be over in moments, and their chance would be lost forever. He stood, frozen in place, unable to do anything except watch. On the boat, the four people greeted one another. The High Priest seemed on good terms with the man, for the man clapped his back and their laughter echoed over the water.

The High Priest gestured at the overflowing basket of goodies, which the thin-man now clasped with both arms. It looked heavy. Smiling, the group ducked into the tent.

To anyone on shore, it appeared to be a small, private evening party.

The servants took up a post on shore, some distance from the boat.

Clearly the men on board wanted privacy to make the transaction. Why else order the servants away? It would also make it impossible for a stranger to get on board, with all four men standing near the gangway.

Two stood guard, facing the city. They were armed with short daggers and clubs, fastened at their waists. The other two sat on the steps. One unfolded a game of Senet, laying the playing board on the ground. When they began throwing knucklebones, the servants standing guard drifted closer to watch.

The red, dusky streaks were fading overhead. Twilight had begun to fall. A huge yellow moon glowed on the horizon. Over the water, an ibis bird flew low and called out in a lonely cry. There was no response.

Zet turned his attention to the boat. On board, inside the tent, lamplight flickered to life. It danced against the white linen walls.

"What are we going to do?" Kat whispered.

"I don't know!"

Zet let out a breath of frustration and sank down with his back to the baskets. He drew his knees up and put his head on his folded arms. What could he do? He was just a single boy. How on earth could he fight four armed servants, and then four more adults if he did somehow miraculously get on board? It was impossible.

"I don't know, Kat," he said again.

"There must be something we can do!"

"Like what?"

She didn't answer.

He'd never thought he could sink so low in life. He never thought a beautiful evening like this could be so disturbing and bleak.

"Zet," Kat said. "Padus will be killed. And Pharaoh too. We're the only people who can stop it. We're the only people who know."

He looked at his sister, whose wide eyes were staring into his own as if searching for an answer. She hadn't even mentioned what would happen to her. It was so like his little sister, to think of everyone else. If a stranger were drowning, she'd throw herself into the river and drown herself trying to save him.

Wait—that was it! He had an idea!

"Kat! Quick. Run for the medjay. Go to the head office if you have to."

"Why? They'll just arrest you!"

"Trust me, just do it."

"Why? What are you going to do?"

"I'm going to get on that boat."

"It's too dangerous."

"Do you have a better suggestion?"

She bit her lip.

"Then run!" he said. "It's our only chance."

She grabbed his wrist. "What if they won't come? What should I tell them?"

"Anything! Tell them I'm trying to murder the High Priest if you have to!"

She let go of him and her hand dropped to her side. Her chin was trembling and she blinked back tears. "All right, I'll do it," she said. She put her arms around his neck in a quick hug. Then she took off running.

Zet turned to face the boat. It was a crazy idea. But with everything lost, it was his only choice left. He'd stop the thieves, he'd free Padus and his family name, and he'd stop the enemies plotting to kill Pharaoh. Or he'd die trying.

CHAPTER 21
ACTION

Keeping one eye on the guards, Zet crept out of his hiding place and made his way to the river. When he reached the water, he slipped in. The bottom felt soft and muddy against the soles of his feet. Silt squished between his toes as he waded toward the water-steps, staying low.

The closer he came, the deeper the water got. Soon he had to tread water to keep his head above the surface. He wasn't the best swimmer, but he managed to dog paddle along with one hand on the wall to guide him.

He kept moving, trying desperately to stay silent. Finally, he reached the first rope that tied the boat to the wharf. Pulling himself up, he risked a peek on shore. The servants were still playing their game of Senet. No one glanced his way, but from this distance their daggers looked longer and sharper, and their arms, muscled from rowing, looked deadly.

The rope had been wound several times around a cleat, and then knotted securely. He worked the knot free, his legs furiously treading water. Then he unwound the rope from the cleat. The rear of the boat floated out a little, but not so far for anyone to notice.

Not yet.

Praying it would stay that way, he swam for the second rope. This went more slowly than the first. The knot was more complicated, and his legs were growing tired. He kept sinking below the surface, and his wet hands were slippery.

On shore, one of the men shouted. Zet looked up, frantic, and saw he was shouting about the game. The shouts were followed by laughter.

The second rope was free.

Zet didn't allow himself time to rest. He tied the rope around his waist and then pushed off the wall with his legs. The current caught hold of the boat and he swam with it, towing the boat from shore. So far so good, but he needed to get to the oars before someone else did.

The polished rail was incredibly slippery. His wet hands found purchase on the bow where the rope had been tied. Feet kicking, he clambered up the hull, climbed over the ledge, and landed with a wet thunk.

He lay, breathing hard, waiting to see if anyone would come investigating.

Someone laughed inside the canopy, and glasses clinked together.

Quietly, he undid the rope from his waist. On hands and knees, Zet crawled forward and found the first oar. He slid it gently over the side. One down, three to go. He found the second and third easily, and worked his way around the tent to find the fourth.

The party inside was seated just on the other side of the thin fabric. His heart pounded. The oar was on its side, and part of the paddle was wedged under the tent. He'd have to pull it out. Zet heard Pharaoh's name mentioned.

"We will see a new Egypt," the High Priest said.

"Indeed," answered a male voice.

Zet got his fingers around the oar and began to slowly pull it toward him.

The man kept talking. "And I presume you'll want more than compensation?"

"Only what Your Eminence deems just, of course," said the High Priest.

The man laughed. "Such modesty does not become you."

He had it. He had the paddle! Zet swung it wide. He didn't mean to let it go so quickly, but it flew out over the water and landed with a splash.

That's when the alarm when up. The servants on the shore shouted. The four people under the enclosed canopy ran out on deck. The High Priest spotted Zet first. His eyes narrowed, but then flew open as recognition dawned.

"You!" he cried.

Zet backed away. He turned, climbed over the rail and jumped into the water.

"Get that boy!" the High Priest shouted.

"Where are my oars?" cried the man next to him. "Get an oar and row!"

Zet was swimming clear of the boat as fast as he could.

"They're in the water," cried the woman. "We're drifting!"

There came the splash of bodies as the four guards on shore plunged into the river. Zet scanned the waterfront, hoping desperately for a glimpse of Kat. The boat had floated out a good distance, but the servants were surprisingly strong swimmers. Zet dogpaddled toward an oar and grabbed hold of it for protection. The instant he had it, though, he knew it would be of little use. It was too unwieldy.

"He's over here! This way," shouted the boat's owner, guiding his men toward Zet's position.

Zet was quickly losing strength. He saw the nearest man approach. Water streamed off the man's thick shoulders. His muscles flexed with each powerful stroke. A scar ran across the man's shaved head, and his nose looked like it had been broken a dozen times.

Maybe if he swam around the boat, the other way! Maybe he could buy some time.

He dogpaddled in terror, glancing back at the man closing in.

The man grinned, showing a mouth full of broken teeth.

"No point, boy," he said.

Zet saw what he meant. Another guard cut across the water from the stern.

The powerful man reached him and they struggled. The servant easily pushed him under, holding him down until Zet thought his lungs would burst. Somehow, he bit the man's arm. Hard. The hand released him.

Zet popped to the surface, gasping, his lungs on fire.

The huge guard grabbed for him again, but Zet found the oar and punched it toward the man's ribs. It hit home so hard the man grunted, momentarily winded.

His score was short lived. From behind, strong arms grabbed him in a headlock and shoved him down. He had barely a second to gulp a mouthful of air before he was pushed under water. He fought, kicking out, knowing every move he made robbed him of precious oxygen. Through the silty water, he could see nothing. Then he felt something hard brush his shoulder. The side of the boat.

With his last burst of life, he kicked free of the man and swam down deep. Using his hands, he felt the underside of the boat, maneuvering himself under it. He needed to breath! By the gods, if he didn't breathe soon, his life would slip away.

He felt a blackness hovering behind his eyes. Water, all around. Warm, liquid death, clasping him in its powerful embrace.

There was no escape.

Without air, there was no life.

CHAPTER 22
UNDER MOONLIGHT

Hands barely aware, they moved upward. Searching. Through his delirium, some part of him knew he'd reached the far side of the boat. He was rising. He could see the surface. The beautiful, shiny surface, with the round yellow moon glowing warmly overhead.

And then he broke through.

Gasping and gasping.

"There he is! There's the rat! Get him!"

With arms like lead, Zet struggled shoreward.

Two men closed around him.

And a whistle sounded from shore.

"This is the medjay!" a man shouted. "I repeat, this is the medjay! Bring the boat in immediately!"

A thick arm wrapped around Zet's torso.

"Not a word," the man growled.

As long as he didn't push Zet under a third time, he was more than willing to comply. He was too exhausted to fight.

"We're drifting!" came the boat owner's reply. "We have no paddles!"

"Stay as you are. We'll come out to you."

There was a hasty argument on board. Meanwhile Zet could see men running down the shore to where several papyrus skiffs had been pulled out of the water. He saw a smaller form in a white short dress, and knew it was Kat. She'd done it. She'd brought medjay. Lots of medjay. With the reflected moonlight, everything looked bright and eerie, a sick, bluish green.

"Forget the boy," said the boat's owner. "Get those paddles and get us out of here!"

The burly servant abandoned Zet, giving him one last shove. Then he and the other men scrambled through the water and pulled themselves on board.

"Hurry! Paddle. They're coming!"

"Stay as you are!" shouted the medjay, powering his skiff through the water.

At this, the boat owner seemed to realize it was no use trying to get away.

"We're trying to row to shore," he called. "A boy sabotaged our party! He threw our oars overboard."

Zet's legs were giving way under him. He swallowed a mouthful of briny water. He couldn't tread much longer.

Two hands grabbed him under his shoulders. He was hauled onto a skiff, his drenched clothes scraping over the woven papyrus. He lay coughing and sputtering.

The medjay who pulled him on board shouted, "You are ordered to stay as you are!"

"We've done nothing wrong! Give us our oars, and let us continue our evening in peace."

"We cannot do that. Your Eminence, we have orders to search your ship. Tell your guards to stand down, or you will all be taken prisoners immediately. We have you surrounded."

And indeed, they did. Zet struggled upright.

The medjay had paddled six skiffs out. Every man was armed with clubs and swords.

When Zet saw the face of the man who'd saved him, he started in shock.

"Merimose!" Zet said in disbelief. "But you were supposed to be—"

"I know." Merimose tapped his skull. "A bit of ingenuity on my part. I wanted them to think I was out of town. I just had no idea where the deal would take place. Thanks to you, we made it."

"So you knew they'd stolen the plans to Pharaoh's palace?"

"Actually, no. But we did get a tip that something like this might be in the works. And we still don't have that precious scroll."

The skiffs had reached the side of the Rose Bark. They tied up along its sloping rail.

"This is an outrage," said the High Priest.

"I'll have you all excommunicated," said the boat's owner. "Do you know who I am?"

"I do, Your Eminence," said Merimose. "And I apologize deeply. But I am under orders to search your ship. And I must do my duty. I'm sure you understand?"

"No. I don't understand. This is my boat. You have no right to come and disturb me!"

"I have every right. I am here on Pharaoh's orders."

And with that, the men swarmed on board.

Zet watched the chaos that ensued. The tent was dismantled. Objects were systematically searched from one end to the other, while the High Priest, the thin-man, and the one they called Your Eminence, stood under guard. The woman cowered in fear near the stern. She'd begun sobbing softly, the beautiful beaded wig hiding her delicate face. Her dress billowed around her like the wings of a caged bird.

Zet saw her hand move, pulling something from the folds of her dress. It was white and rolled into a tight scroll, and blended with her clothing so well he couldn't quite understand what she was doing. She leaned closer to the rail, her other hand over her sobbing face.

"She has it!" Zet shouted. "The girl!"

Everyone turned.

The girl was no longer sobbing. Instead she stood and flung the papyrus as hard as she could out over the water.

With his last burst of strength, Zet dove in after it. Barely a corner had touched the surface when he grabbed hold and lifted the thick paper skyward. He struggled back to the skiff and climbed on board. He had to see. He had to make sure.

He found a cloth on the bottom of the boat and dried his hands. Then, holding one edge carefully so as not to drip on it, he unrolled the papyrus just one hand's width. He stared down at the black, neatly made diagram. Even from what he could see, it was obviously huge and detailed, with numbers and floor plans. He recognized the front entrance, where he'd stood and tried to speak to Pharaoh. It was, without doubt, the complete layout of the Great One's palace.

"This is it!" Zet shouted.

On board, Merimose ordered the three men and the woman bound.

"What is this? We've done nothing wrong!"

"You are under arrest for treason, and conspiring to kill the Pharaoh."

CHAPTER 23
WHEN CAMELS FLY

They'd done it. They'd truly done it. Zet whooped as waves of relief washed over him. On shore, his sister was leaping from foot to foot. She screamed with joy when Zet stumbled, dripping, onto the water-steps.

"Good job," he told her. "You did it. You brought them."

"I'm sorry it took so long! I couldn't find anyone! They'd all gone to the temple. They had it surrounded. They wouldn't come away!"

Merimose approached. "Not until Kat told me she was your sister," he said. "Then we came running. That's for sure."

"So does that mean I'll get my reward?" Zet asked. He sure needed it!

The medjay laughed. He clapped Zet on the back. "I misjudged you. Clearly, I shouldn't have set the price so high! I should've known a persistent one like you wouldn't stop until he got his pay." But the man was smiling from ear to ear. "Of course you will. I'll be happy to pay it. You and your sister here deserve every bit of it. Come tomorrow morning. I'll be waiting."

"Actually, there's one more favor I have to ask," Zet said.

Merimose glanced skyward. "Oh no. Here we go with the

bargaining. I never was much good at bargaining." But he was grinning. "Go ahead."

"It's about a friend of ours. He was arrested earlier today." Zet told Merimose about Padus.

Merimose nodded. "I'm on my way. He'll be free within the hour."

"We better go too. We need to find our mother," Zet said. "She's waiting for us." And then, realizing how good it sounded, he added, "We need to go home."

It was a happy reunion when they returned to the Hearing Ear Chapel and told their mother they were safe. She was proud when she learned that Zet and Kat had stopped a plot to kill Pharaoh, and added that their father, a fighting soldier himself, couldn't ask for anything better for Egypt.

The only thing Zet and Kat hadn't told her about was the ruined stall. They'd be getting their reward, but it would be nowhere near enough to buy back the stock they'd lost. They'd have to start small. It was going to be a hard road, especially given the times.

The following morning, their mother insisted Zet and Kat dress in their finest to accept the reward. So, cleaned and wearing a fresh linen tunic, Zet headed out the door. Beside him, Kat's hair shone in two thick black plaits, and she wore a white dress with a colored sash around her waist and her mother's necklace made of painted wooden beads.

They giggled at the sight of each other.

"I feel stupid," Zet said.

"And I feel pretty. Come on, let's run!"

At the head office, they stepped up the stairs and through the door. A cheer went up. Everywhere Zet looked, men in uniform were on their feet, clapping. People stepped forward to congratulate the two of them. Zet's heart swelled with relief. He and his sister shared a glance of amazement.

Merimose bowed low and handed them the deben.

"I may not have seen a camel fly," Merimose said, "But I have witnessed bravery that was even more astonishing. This will not be forgotten. Thank you."

When they finally left, Zet felt as if he were humming with gratitude. They'd survived. They walked through the streets. There was someone they needed to visit.

Before long, the familiar curtain came into view.

Padus stood outside on the stoop. He wore his mismatched sandals. His face spread into a huge grin at the sight of them. The three piled inside, and Zet and Kat took turns telling what happened after Padus had been hauled away.

Ama brought tea and bread.

"And what happened in jail? Did they hurt you?" Kat wanted to know.

"I was fine. They held me in a room, but so much effort was being put into the search that the men mostly ignored me."

Zet took out the bag with the reward. "That reminds me. We wanted to share this with you. Because if it wasn't for your help, we'd be dead. And if it wasn't for me seeing you that day, we'd never have this at all."

Padus shook his head and held up a calloused hand. "I won't hear of it!"

"No, children," Ama said. "We are fine. And you have your stall to think of."

"Well, there is someone else then, that we want to give some of the reward to," Zet said.

Padus raised his brows, curious.

"The old woman by your field," Kat said.

"Old woman?" Padus looked puzzled. "What old woman?"

"The blind one. She stays out by the entrance."

"I've never seen a blind woman by my field."

Now it was Zet and Kat's turn to look puzzled.

"But she was there, twice. We visited her." Zet stood. "We'd better go now to find her. Maybe she's already wandering somewhere else. I'd hate to miss her."

Taking their leave, they headed out the door. Zet and Kat made their way mostly in silence. There was so much to think about. So much had happened, it felt like months had passed, rather than just a few short days.

They left the city behind and wandered along the dirt road. Soon the papyrus stand came into view, tall and weaving in the gentle breeze.

The depression in the grass where they'd sat with the old woman still remained, but there was no sign of her. Together they wandered up the road for some time, searching, hoping desperately to find her. No one had seen her. No one remembered the blind old woman who'd been so kind to Zet and Kat.

Kat brushed away a few tears. "I so wanted to find her."

"I know," Zet said. "I did too. We'll come looking again. Maybe she'll turn up."

Despite the joy they'd felt, they headed home with heavy hearts. Zet hated to think of the woman, alone somewhere.

They were met by a commotion in their alley. It seemed like hundreds of guards filled the street, although there may have only been twenty or thirty. A beautifully decorated litter lay outside their front door. Next to it, a dozen litter bearers stood at attention.

Zet and Kat eyed them in astonishment, and ran up the front steps.

CHAPTER 24
AN UNEXPECTED GUEST

Inside, their mother looked flushed and breathless. She sat at their dinner table, and cups had been laid out. Across the table, seated on Zet's plump cushion, sat the little old woman. Instead of rags, however, she was dressed in royal colors. A sumptuous gown flowed from her thin shoulders.

"Is that you, children?" she said, turning her blind eyes toward them.

"Yes," said Zet. "But you are—"

"The Royal Mother. Yes. Come, sit by me and I will explain."

She told them of how she'd feared for her son's life. She'd heard the rumors, and had sent her men everywhere, but no one knew for certain who led the plot. She'd had the High Priest followed. And so, when she learned the High Priest had gone to the field and met the thin-man, she asked to be brought there herself, that night. She too believed they might come back to cover their tracks, and she wanted to confront them herself.

"But I met you instead!" she said.

"Why did you come back and eat with us the next day?" Kat cried. "You are the Royal Mother, and we are just children."

"I couldn't turn down such a kind offer," she said softly.

And he knew she meant it.

"When I said you'd made me a happy woman, I meant it. That was one of the loveliest days in memory."

They reminisced about it, telling their mother how they'd eaten bowls of leftovers. Their mother laughed, amazed.

"You are a good cook!" the Royal Mother said. "I've still been dreaming of that chickpea salad. You'll have to give me the recipe!"

"Still, it wasn't safe," Zet said. "What if someone recognized you?"

"My guards were all around me. Hidden in the field."

Zet shook his head, amazed. "But why didn't you just arrest the thin-man. Or the High Priest? Or search the temple? Why wait?"

"How could we? The High Priest cannot be touched by regular laws. And how could we accuse him? On what evidence? He was a very cunning man. As for the thin-man, there seemed to be little point. It was better to let him go. We hoped he would lead us to some kind of answer. The only way we could succeed was to catch the High Priest in the act."

The morning passed swiftly, with much talk and laughter. Baby Apu crawled around, gurgling his delight at all the happy people.

Finally, the Royal Mother said it was time for her to get back to her son at the Palace.

Zet helped her up.

"My son and I will be forever grateful," she said, squeezing his hands.

The family went outside to see her off. People crowded the streets, unable to believe a Royal visitor had come to the house of a market family. They watched in awe as Zet and Kat and their mother said goodbye.

Seated in the litter, the Royal Mother took Zet and Kat's hands in her small, wrinkled ones.

"I know you suffered great struggles. But you did the right thing. I will never forget this. And neither will my son."

Zet watched her go, barely able to believe that the kind woman they'd shared lunch with was the same great lady who rode in a litter surrounded by dozens of guards.

He trailed after his family, up the steps and into the front room.

"What's that?" he asked his mother, seeing a box near the front door.

"The Great Mother brought it for you. I don't know, I'd forgotten all about it."

"I wonder what it is?" He and Kat went to it and knelt before it.

The box was beautifully carved, inlaid with gold and turquoise and bore the Pharaoh's mark.

"This box must be worth a fortune!" Zet said.

"Open it," Kat cried.

And he did. He lifted the lid and gasped. On top was a small piece of papyrus, with a neatly printed note. Beneath the note lay a shining mound of deben. Kat took out the note and read it.

"For goods lost in the line of duty. Please accept with our thanks," she read. "And it's signed by Pharaoh himself!"

Zet thought of the man he'd seen with the dark eyes, and closed his own eyes in thanks.

Their business was saved. Pharaoh knew, and understood. He'd taken the time to find out what Zet had gone through, and what he'd lost. And what lay inside this box was beyond generous. They could easily buy back their pots. And they wouldn't have to worry about starving for a long time.

"Goods lost in the line of duty?" his mother said.

"Uh . . ." Zet looked at his sister. "Do you want to explain?"

"No way!" she said.

They both turned to their mother, who was studying their faces.

"All right children. Just what goods, exactly, are we talking about?"

And so they told her about the stall, and even about the three favorite bowls he'd lost in the chase. It's true, she was upset, but in the end they organized a wonderful trip down river to visit the village where the potters made their beautiful wares.

It took several boats to bring their haul back to town.

The stall looked incredible when it was done. Everything was new and fresh.

They even had little toys made of clay.

"I'm so glad everything's back to normal, aren't you?" Zet asked his sister.

"That's for sure," she said. "I hope nothing like that happens ever again. Don't you?"

At that moment, a medjay ran into square. His insignia shone at his throat, and his sword and club banged at his hip. He looked this way and that, and then beelined for the stall.

"Are you the boy called Zet?"

"I am."

"Merimose sent me. He wondered if you'd like to make a little extra deben?"

Zet and Kat glanced at each other.

Zet shrugged at his sister, and was unable to keep the grin from his face. "It couldn't hurt, if it's for a good cause, right?"

She rolled her eyes. "May the gods protect us."

"Hurry!" the man said.

"I'm on my way," Zet replied. And together, they took off into the sunlit afternoon.

HISTORICAL NOTE FROM THE AUTHOR

This story is a work of fiction. While none of the characters mentioned actually existed, the setting is very much as it would have been during the time when this book was set. Little remains of the old city of Thebes beyond the great monuments. Certain places however, such as the Temple of Amenemopet with its forest of stone pillars, can actually be visited today.

The Egyptians kept very good notes. They loved to write things down. Using their records we can imagine what life was like—from their clothing to the marketplaces, from their foods to their customs. Most families kept a household shrine and Bastet, the cat deity, was a popular household god. Citizens did not visit temples in the way churches are visited today. Only priests were allowed inside. The Hearing Ear shrines were a great way for people to make requests of their gods.

The medjay began as additional troops during wartime, but evolved into a more regular police force. Crimes were tried in court, as they are today, but the punishments could often be brutal. The best a thief could hope for was the loss of a hand. The worst was burning at the stake, a terrible fate for an Egyptian; they believed that destroying their body in this way meant that they would not go on to lead an afterlife.

~

DOWNLOAD THE STUDY GUIDE
FOR MYSTERY OF THE EGYPTIAN SCROLL

Available at *bit.ly/egyptstudy*

~

PLEASE ACCEPT MY HEARTFELT THANKS
IN ADVANCE IF YOU
REVIEW THIS ON AMAZON

ACKNOWLEDGEMENTS AND SOURCES

So much goes into writing a book. I couldn't have done it without the help of the following amazing people. First, I must thank my parents, who have always gone above and beyond to support and encourage me. My thanks goes out to Peter and Judy Wyshynski, to my sisters Jill and Sarah, to Scott Lisetor, Sharon Brown, Amanda Budde-Sung, Ellie Crowe, Adria Estribou, Glenn Desy, and David Desy. And to everyone who had a hand in this novel, and who helped me along the way, I say thank you from the bottom of my heart.

Further thanks to the following sources:
Romer, J, 'Ancient Lives: The Story of the Pharaoh's Tombmakers', Weidenfeld & Nicolson, 1984
Booth, C, 'Ancient Egypt: Thebes and the Nile Valley In The Year 1200 BCE', Quid 2008
Casson, L, 'Everyday Life in Ancient Egypt, Revised and Expanded Edition', John Hopkins University Press, 2001
Brier, B, PHD, 'The Murder of Tutankhamen', G. P. Putnam's Sons, 1998

Morell, V, 'The Pyramid Builders', National Geographic Nov. 2001

Fletcher, J, 'The Egyptian Book of Living and Dying', Duncan Baird 2002

Oakes, L and Gahlin, L, 'Ancient Egypt, An illustrated reference to the myths, religions, pyramids and temples of the land of the pharaohs', Anness Publishing 2003

Muller and Thiem, 'Gold of the Pharaohs', Sterling, 2005

Klum, M, 'King Cobras, Revered and Feared', National Geographic Nov. 2001

ALSO BY SCOTT PETERS

The Complete Zet Mystery Series

Mystery of the Egyptian Scroll

Mystery of the Egyptian Amulet

Mystery of the Egyptian Temple

Mystery of the Egyptian Mummy

More Great Ancient Egypt Reads

Secret of the Egyptian Curse

Mummies: 101 Ancient Egypt Mummy Facts

The I Escaped Series

I Escaped North Korea!

I Escaped The California Camp Fire

I Escaped the World's Deadliest Shark Attack

I Escaped Amazon River Pirates

FIND OUT ABOUT NEW BOOKS

www.subscribepage.com/scottpeters

VISIT MY WEBSITE FOR TONS OF

ANCIENT EGYPT FACTS AND ACTIVITIES!

www.kidsancientegypt.com

Printed in Great Britain
by Amazon

53085153R00069